To Ben
Merry Christmas
2002/03
David Bany

Each Man Kills

DAVID BARRY

First Impression—2002

ISBN 1 84323 082 8

© David Barry 2002

This book is published with the support of the
Arts Council of Wales.

Printed in Wales by
Gomer Press, Llandysul, Ceredigion

To
Emma
and
Morgan

Yet each man kills the thing he loves,
By each let this be heard,
Some do it with a bitter look,
Some with a flattering word,
The coward does it with a kiss,
The brave man with a sword!

From *The Ballad of Reading Gaol* by Oscar Wilde

Chapter 1

Raindrops trickled across the lilies like tears. Were they lilies? Lambert wasn't certain. Flowers had never been his strong point. He felt his arm being touched sympathetically, and a voice of condolence, heavy with theatrical emotion, said: 'He was a good bloke, Harry. A good bloke.'

Even if he did treat my mother like shit, Lambert thought.

He chased the thought away and nodded slightly, his face expressionless, then looked up from the ragged display of wilting flowers and bouquets. Through the small throng of mourners that circled him he caught sight of Helen, standing slightly apart from the rest of the mourners, her pale attractive face outlined by the black umbrella she was holding. It crossed his mind that it was just like Helen to do the right thing. Even though she had disliked his father, she would never have considered turning up at his funeral with a coloured umbrella.

He nodded at some of the mourners as he brushed past them and crossed to where she stood. He noticed the grey had gone from her hair and it was now uniformly black. She gave him a sympathetic smile as he approached.

He coughed delicately before speaking. 'Thanks for coming.'

'The least I could do,' she replied softly, looking up at him, staring deep into his eyes, searching for the way he felt. It was a sympathetic moment which was broken when she dropped her gaze to the tie he wore, brash and loud.

He affected not to notice her disapproval and looked up at the sky with a wry smile. 'Rain's appropriate,' he said, immediately regretting the cliché.

'It'll stop soon,' she said. 'It's only a shower.'

'Where's Natasha?' he asked, though he knew damn well where she was. And, more to the point, why she wasn't here.

'You know very well. She's got her finals.'

'I would have thought she'd want to be here.'

Helen sniffed, and her mouth twitched slightly into that pinched look he found unattractive. 'She'd not had much to do with your father for a long time.'

'All the same,' he said. He realised it sounded weak but could think of nothing to add and remained silent. He welcomed the sudden intrusion of one of the mourners, who grabbed his hand to shake, pumping it almost too enthusiastically.

'He'll be missed down The Eagle. We'll push the boat out for him tonight. Think you can make it, Harry?'

Before replying to the beefy, red-faced mourner, Lambert glanced towards Helen, who looked away quickly, to avoid him seeing her expression of disapproval.

Lambert gave the mourner a conspiratorial grin. 'I'm not sure about tonight. I'll have to see.' He inclined his head towards the crematorium gates. 'You coming back for a bite to eat and a drink, Steve?'

'Yeah but – sorry – I can't stay long. Got to shoot over to Port Talbot later.'

'No problem. See you back there, Steve.'

The mourner made a sideways mouth-clicking sound at Lambert, as if he was a small boy, then turned and walked purposefully towards the crematorium gates. Lambert watched him for a moment then turned back towards Helen, feeling he had to explain.

'You know ... there was never anything ... anything dodgy about Dad's relationship with Natasha.'

'I never said there was.'

'You didn't have to. He wouldn't have touched her, you know. Never.'

Helen's mouth tightened. 'No, but the way he used to look at her. I swear . . .' She checked herself and looked round at the Garden of Remembrance. 'I'm sorry. He's gone now. Does it matter?'

Lambert gazed into her eyes, probing. 'It matters to me. You coming back for some grub?'

'Do you really want me to?'

'Maybe we could go out after. For a drink. To talk.'

Helen gave him a crooked smile. 'Neutral ground?'

'Something like that.'

'All right then.'

Lambert grinned. He felt the burden of grief leaving his body and his eyes gained a slight sparkle. Perhaps there was a ghost of a chance to mend the relationship.

*　　　　　*　　　　　*

Gary Evans chucked the ball of stale chewing gum into the wastebin and fed a fresh piece into his mouth. He returned to the sofa and picked up the Browning Automatic, weighing it thoughtfully, as if he was about to pose in firing position, aiming at an imaginary adversary. But Gary Evans was too experienced to indulge in games. He was for real. Pretend was for amateurs.

The phone rang. He placed the gun hurriedly but carefully next to the Armalite rifle on the sofa, and snatched the phone from the glass coffee table in the middle of the room. He was expecting the call and braced himself for bad news. He breathed a small sigh of relief when he heard the voice at the other end.

'Oh, it's you, Terry.'

But he was also disappointed. He would just have to sit tight and wait for the inevitable to happen. He checked his watch as Terry Clark demanded they meet urgently at a country pub.

'OK,' he agreed. 'I'll be there. But listen, I'd sooner stay in Swansea and . . .'

Terry had already hung up. It was just like him. Say what he had to, then get off the phone. It was all part of Terry's pose. That's what Gary Evans hated about his mate. He was a poser. And posers tend to take unnecessary risks. Still, Terry had never fucked up badly. He was still in one piece and that's what counted in this game.

Evans checked his watch again before wrapping the guns in protective plastic and hiding them back under the floorboards. He sighed as he laid the carpet back into place. Why did it have to be Terry who'd rung? Why not the hospital? He'd been dreading the call, but he wanted it to be over.

Before leaving, he diverted his calls to his mobile, which he clipped to the belt of his 501s. He paused at the door, looking back at his living room with a trace of regret, as if he might never return. Even though the room lacked personality, it had been comforting to know he had his own refuge, somewhere he could shut himself away. His flat was sparse, but he liked it that way. The walls were painted midnight blue, which gave him a deep sense of nocturnal restfulness. There were no pictures on any of the walls, the only adornment being the dominating presence of an enormous horse's head mask, a reproduction Celtic chariot shield that stared down with lifeless gaping eyes. The rest of the room revealed little of the character of its occupant. That's what he liked. Clean-cut simplicity, sharp as a six-inch blade. What was that word Terry had used? Minimalist. That was it. Trust Terry to know poncey bloody words like that.

*　　　　*　　　　*

As he paid for the drinks, Lambert glanced towards the table where Helen was sitting. He saw her rummaging through her handbag for her lipstick. He watched as she repainted

12

her lips and savoured the moment. He had missed her familar ways, the comforting touches and gestures of years of intimacy; he felt dryness in his throat, a moistness behind the eyes.

He carried the drinks over, wondering what to say to her now that she'd agreed to meet him. He felt lost, an inarticulate teenager. Not that he'd been inarticulate in his teens. That was half his problem. He'd always had the gift of the gab where women were concerned.

She looked up as he put down the drinks and sat opposite her. He tried to analyse the look. Resignation? It seemed to convey emptiness. He was looking into the eyes of a victim and he was the perpetrator. He raised his pint glass, smiling feebly, and toasted her in Welsh.

'Iechyd da!'

She raised her glass slowly, but held it close to herself to avoid any toast. This meeting was no celebration, she wanted him to know that. She wanted him to suffer, even if it only meant being deprived of all those shared responses from their past.

Evading the expected response, she said, 'Cheers' instead, and it came out superciliously English, as though she looked down on the Welsh. She hadn't meant it to sound that way. She loved the Welsh, and she had loved her Welshman. Only now her feelings were coloured by experience. She realised she had been in love with an ideal, a culture eroded by the permissive, 'enlightened' decades. The Welshmen of her generation seemed to be boozers or lechers or both. She longed for a past she had never known. Hymn-singing chapel, fire and brimstone preachers, and temperance societies.

She sipped her white wine and winced. Acid like her mood. Why on earth had she agreed to meet her ex-husband like this? It was a mistake. What was she doing here? She glanced around at the cosy, false atmosphere of this recently

13

built, architectural-salvage, hybrid Victorian/Tudor pub, shelves lined with old books no one would ever read, and wondered if he'd brought anyone else here.

'How d'you know this place?' she said.

Lambert knew what she was driving at and assumed a faithful, dog-like expression. 'Been here before. Once, with my sergeant, on our way back from an investigation.'

She nodded slowly, mulling it over, then sipped her wine.

Lambert studied her carefully before speaking. 'I miss you, you know.'

'I miss you, too,' she said automatically, and immediately regretted it, resenting him, as if he'd forced it out of her. She knew exactly what he would say next.

'So what's the problem?'

She gave him a pained expression.

'Look,' he continued, ignoring it. 'I know I behaved like a shit, but . . .'

She flared up. 'Oh, let's just let bygones be bygones, why don't we? Forget about the used condom I found on the back seat of your car.' She shuddered at the memory.

'I've told you, I was so pissed I can't remember.'

Helen gave him an icy smile. 'But not so drunk you forgot to take precautions.'

'Look, Helen, we've been over this . . .' he began. 'Don't you think I'd like to wind the clock back?'

'So you could clear up the mess behind you, inspector? Harry, your priority is don't get caught or admit to anything. Isn't that the police code?'

'Criminal, actually.'

'It's a thin dividing line.'

Lambert frowned. That he was an honest copper there was never any doubt. But he suddenly felt unsure of himself. Had he given Helen the impression over the years that he was corrupt? After all, as far as she was concerned, he had shown himself to be untrustworthy.

He downed most of his pint before responding. 'Did you come out here just to have another go at me?' It came out sounding pathetic and he waited for her next onslaught.

'No, I don't know. I . . . I just wish things could change.' She stared at him with a mixture of defeat and bitterness, sighing deeply. Then she spat out with sudden venom, 'You're just like your fucking father.'

'Steady on. We've only just buried him.'

He wasn't used to her swearing and felt he had been wrong-footed.

'I couldn't give a toss,' she went on. 'Look how he treated your mother when she was alive. Bastard.'

Lambert smiled thinly. 'It runs in the family.'

Suddenly tired of their meeting, Helen stared at him wearily, then her eyes dropped to his chest.

'And as for that tie,' she said.

*   *   *

Terry was sitting on a stool by the bar when Evans arrived at the pub. 'There you go, mate.' He handed Evans a bottle of Budweiser and looked at his watch. 'I've only just got here myself.'

'Cheers.' Evans took the bottle, frowning. 'I didn't want to leave Swansea right now, Terry. I was hoping we could've met somewhere in town.'

'Nah, shitholes them pubs.'

Evans suddenly felt impatient, irritated by his friend's flash attitude. 'OK,' he said. 'What's on your mind?'

Grinning, Terry leaned closer to him. 'We've had a call from the Avenue.'

Evans noticed the awe, the undisguised admiration for covert power, that Terry carried in his voice.

Terry's grin grew bigger and cockier. 'Fuckin' A, Mac!' he said loudly in a mock American dialect. A middle-aged man, ordering drinks at the bar, glanced at his wife apologetically before glaring pointedly at Terry, who stared back confrontationally. 'Sorry, pal. Didn't mean to upset the *lady wife.*'

The man found Terry's bullet-shaped, cropped head and smugly arrogant expression intimidating. Feigning embarrassment, he studied the coins in his hand, while Terry continued staring at him for a moment, as if fighting the urge to beat him to a pulp. Evans sighed impatiently. He knew it was all part of Terry's act. Terry was still a pro and attacking a civilian was not a smart way to operate. Not unless you want to jeopardise the next job by risking a custodial sentence for GBH.

'What do they want us to do?' Evans asked as Terry turned to look at him, grinning.

Terry dropped his voice again. 'Job for the Israelis. And no problems with the Foreign Office. Piece of piss, this one. Dangerous, but no political complications.'

Evans swigged from his bottle and unthinkingly touched the mobile phone on his hip, willing it to ring.

'Yeah, this one's kosher,' Terry laughed. 'Got the ministry seal of approval. And it pays. Shit does it pay.'

Evans took a deep breath. The stale smell of cigars and cigarettes caught in his throat and he took a long swig of beer before speaking. 'I might not be able to handle this one. Not now.'

Terry leaned forward on his stool. 'What d'you mean, you can't handle it?'

'Not now. Bad time.'

Terry patted his arm understandingly. 'Look, I know it's risky, man, but we've been in some tight spots before.'

'It isn' that.'

'What then?'

'Call it compassionate leave. She isn' gonna make it, Terry. So I've gorra stay. It's as simple as that.'

Terry sighed. 'Listen, mate, this caper ain't for two, maybe three, weeks. S'posing she snuffs it in the next couple of days?'

Evans's jaw tightened. He brushed his hand several times hard against his close-cropped hair.

'Gary, listen, I only meant . . .' Terry started to explain, but was interrupted by a mobile phone playing an unrecognisable tune. He instinctively reached for his own phone which he had left in front of him on top of the bar, before realising it was Gary's. Evans was already unclipping his phone from his belt and walking towards the door leading to the toilets to answer the call.

*   *   *

Lambert made a mock, exaggerated show of searching for his own mobile as he heard the phone ringing from the other side of the bar. It was a way to break the awkward silence into which they had both descended.

'It's OK,' he reassured her. 'I left it in the car.'

She shrugged and sniffed, and he wondered if she was going to cry. He cleared his throat gently before asking her, 'So why *did* you come out here with me?'

She looked deep into his eyes, wanting him to see the bitterness and disappointment that would be with her now for the rest of her life. 'Just searching for the mysterious Welshman I once knew.'

Perhaps it was delayed reaction from his father's funeral, but Lambert, who was usually sensitive to the moods of others, chose to ignore the signals she was sending out and made light of the situation. 'Mysterious Wales,' he scoffed. 'Wizards and witches. Fairies, superstitions and a load of bollocks.'

Helen smiled a cold, humourless smile of resignation. 'Just as I thought,' she said. 'There's nothing left, is there? Nothing to patch. Nothing to mend.'

As if seeing him for the last time, she cast her eyes over his lived-in face. He was ruggedly good looking, with an overtly masculine cleft chin, soft blue eyes and cherubic, sensual lips. She still found him attractive, and it angered her, knowing she was chained forever to the past.

'I may have done many things,' Lambert began, trying to sound remorseful. 'Morally reprehensible, terrible things. And, God knows, I've treated you badly, but I just want you to know that I've never – *never* – done anything in my work that was dishonest. I've never taken any bribes or planted evidence . . .'

Irritated, Helen interrupted him. 'Why is it so important to you, telling me this? Why d'you think it would interest me now?'

He shrugged helplessly. 'I suppose I just want you to know that at least I'm not a complete and total shit. It's important to me because of all the good times we had together. All the memories we share.'

'Listen, Detective Inspector Double Standards, you've destroyed those memories. Killed them off. And I couldn't care less if you get some poor bugger wrongfully arrested and locked up for life just to further your career. I'm not interested.'

'You don't mean that.'

Helen sighed deeply and looked at her empty glass. 'Seeing as you're driving, I'll have another.'

Lambert felt he was being wrong-footed again. Why did Helen want to prolong this meeting if there was no hope of a reconciliation? Perhaps it was just so that she could put the boot in. Well, he decided, he would play along. He owed her that much. Wasn't this restorative justice, where the culprit is confronted by the victim? Or was he just indulging himself, allowing himself to wallow in remorse?

As only we Welsh know how, he thought as he rose from the table.

18

He ordered another wine for Helen and a half of bitter for himself. He glanced at his watch. It was past two-thirty. He'd drunk two glasses of wine after the funeral and had just downed a pint of bitter. He calculated the units of alcohol, measured them against the time, and decided if he had another half he would be within the legal limits. Just.

Further along the bar, Evans rejoined his colleague, clipping his mobile back on his belt.

'Bad news?' Terry asked.

Evans ignored him and swigged back the last of his beer.

'We've got loads of time, if you wanna change your mind,' Terry persisted.

Evans shook his head. 'I can't make any plans. I've got to go. I'll see you. Take it easy.'

He slammed his Budweiser bottle on the bar, hurriedly crossed towards the exit and collided forcefully with Lambert, causing him to spill his beer. He carried on walking, without bothering to apologise.

Lambert responded automatically. 'Hey!'

But Evans was already out of the door.

*   *   *

Morris James drove his Skoda carefully through Swansea, never going over twenty miles an hour. He was worried about Sadie. She'd been depressed lately. He was reluctant to leave her on her own. But she insisted that he did the usual weekly shop, which he always did on his own, and so he had driven down to Sainsbury's on the Marina. He liked it down on the Marina. It was his little bolthole. Often, when he went to do the weekly shop, he would leave the car in Sainsbury's car park, and before going into the store would permit himself half an hour wandering round the Marina, looking at the boats, or strolling along the beach by the observatory. But not today. Today he dashed straight into the store and bought the bare essentials, allowing himself no time to ponder the fancier produce. It had still taken him over an hour to get down there, park and do the shopping.

A Ford Escort drove too close behind him. Climbing a hill, the Skoda slowed to fifteen miles an hour. The pounding, pulsating beat from the Escort's stereo aggravated the young driver's frustration and he flashed his headlights and blasted his horn. But Morris James was unmoved by the action and merely tutted to himself. He turned slowly into his street and the Escort driver carried straight on, over-compensating on the acceleration now that the Skoda was out of his way.

The James's ramshackle, two-storey, terraced house, was perched halfway up a steep street of similarly neglected houses, as if the neighbours had a pact not to outdo one another. Morris parked the car, leaving it in gear, and took the four bags of shopping from the boot, struggling to carry two in each hand to save himself a journey. As he pushed his key into the front door, one of the shopping bags tipped over, spilling its contents over the front step. Awkwardly, because his knee was giving him gyp, he bent down and picked up a chocolate Swiss roll and tub of margarine, and rescued a tin of baked beans as it started to roll down the step.

'I'm back,' he called out as he kicked the front door shut behind him. Another twinge of pain shot through his knee. He stopped in the dark hallway and listened, recovering from his exertions. Although he was only forty-eight, Morris James was out of condition and got out of breath easily. He was asthmatic.

'Sadie?' he called once more, before taking the shopping into the kitchen and starting to unpack. Again, not for the first time today, he felt there was something wrong. It was unsettling and it had to do with the silence of the house. Usually Sadie had the radio on. She liked listening to the Talk FM station, people airing their dirty laundry in public.

He listened to the faint tick of the kitchen clock, suddenly significant as it heightened the eerie feeling of pervading quiet in the house. He hurried back into the hall.

'Sadie? Where are you?'

He rushed into the front room and stopped, his eyes immediately drawn to a glass tumbler precariously perched on a corner of the coffee table. His heart sank. He sniffed the glass and shivered. Then, with a frenzy bordering on mania, he began searching the room, pulling open drawers, scattering old newspapers and ransacking the bookshelves. He found what he was searching for under the seat of an old leather armchair. An empty vodka bottle.

'Oh, Sadie,' he moaned quietly, suddenly drained. Wearily, he took the vodka bottle, went out into the hall and began to climb the stairs. He knew now what he would find. Ashamed of her disease, she always crawled away like a wounded animal to the small room on the top floor, a dusty room filled with junk.

His knee pained him as he climbed the first flight of stairs and he started limping. All he could hear was his own heavy breathing, wheezing asthmatically.

'Oh, Sadie, Sadie,' he began to blubber. The vodka bottle clattered against the stair rail. He rounded the corner of the first floor and started to climb the flight to the top. He stopped suddenly. The shadow which lay before him on the musty old stair carpet was black and menacing. He looked up. The vodka bottle slipped from his fingers and smashed into the hall below.

He stared at her legs, lifeless and still, dangling in the air.

He followed the line of her body upwards, hardly daring to breathe in the stillness of the afternoon. She had hanged herself, he noted, with the blue towelling cord from his dressing gown.

21

Chapter 2

The staff nurse smiled at Evans and nodded towards the mobile attached to his belt. 'Is that switched off?' He stared at her for a moment, trying to comprehend what she was asking him. 'Your mobile,' she repeated.

'Oh, yes. Sorry.' He switched it off then looked towards the green curtains drawn around his mother's bed. 'How is she?'

'She's comfortable. But we don't think she's got very long.'

Evans stared at her with sudden intensity. 'Has she spoken? Said anything?'

'It's doubtful. But I've not long been on duty. I'll ask sister, if you like.'

'Don't bother,' said Evans.

The nurse felt herself reddening and snatched a look at her watch. She licked the dryness from her lips and composed herself. Evans, noticing her discomfort, added in a softer, more apologetic tone, 'Okay if I go in and see her now?'

'Of course. Stay as long as you like.'

She tugged the curtains back gently and he slipped between the gap. He froze. He had been seeing his mother regularly like this for the past three weeks, but it was still a shock. It was hard to believe she was only in her mid-forties. She looked like an old woman: her hair white, her face emaciated and her head already a lifeless skull. He wondered if it was too late to tell her how he felt about her. Would she be able to hear him? Or was she too close to death?

'Can I get you anything?' the nurse whispered at his side.

He shook his head slightly without taking his eyes off his mother. He felt the curtains fall back into place as the nurse drifted quietly away and he eased himself into a chair beside the bed and took his mother's hand. It was cold. Although it was stifling in the ward, her hand felt lifeless and frozen. He was used to death. But this was different. This slow, agonising wait.

A raucous, phlegmy cough, followed by a spitting sound, came from a bed nearby, and from a far corner of the ward an elderly patient demanded a bedpan. Evans felt angry. He had seen death at close quarters, staring it in the face. But it was a soldier's death. It had its own righteous beauty. Not like his mother's lingering, inglorious end.

He wanted to cry but all he felt was a sort of dazed numbness. He tried squeezing her hand to see if there was the slightest feeling, awareness of his presence, but there was nothing. He looked at her eyes, wondering if they might ever open again, flicker for just a brief moment, but there was no movement. They remained absolutely still. But as he watched, her eyelids began twitching rapidly and her lips began to move. He moved across the bed quickly and put his ear close to her mouth. Her lips were scorchingly dry, like old leather. He felt a slight tingling sensation, the last clinging to life as a hoarse rasping came from somewhere deep inside her. She was trying to tell him something.

'Mum. Mum. It's me. Gary.'

He put his ear close to her mouth again and listened, feeling her lips moving. She knew he was there. She was speaking to him, telling him what he wanted to hear.

As he drew away from her, the tenderness he had felt a moment ago was gone. Now there was an icy glint in his eye, a ruthless determination behind his blank expression. He stood up straight, almost to attention, and spoke quietly.

'All things whatsoever ye would that men should do to you, do ye even so to them.'

23

He watched his mother, waiting, knowing she would die peacefully now. It took less than a minute. Her throat rattled. That was all. Followed by a final stillness. Then, without looking back at her lifeless form, he pushed his way through the curtains and left the ward, his Nike trainers squeaking across the polished floor.

'Mr Evans?' the staff nurse called after him. She watched his retreating figure marching purposefully away from her along the corridor. He was so obviously a squaddie, it was written all over him. And usually, those young soldiers were bad news. Still, he was not bad looking. Boyish good looks, falling just short of being stunningly handsome; his nose was perhaps just a bit too wide and his eyes were on the small side, sunk back into his face, giving him a slightly stark appearance. But quite fanciable. She and her friend Sylvia had discussed him in the staff canteen, jokingly sharing their sexual fantasies with unsuppressed intimacy.

With a sigh she moved towards Mrs Evans's bed and parted the curtains. Right away she knew she was dead. She frowned as she thought about the son. Something told her that he had washed his hands of her, that he would not be returning to pick up her effects or make arrangements for the funeral.

*   *   *

Lambert was distracted by a bluebottle hurling itself at the bare wall of the Interview Room. He wanted to get up and either kill it or let it escape. Anything to stop the manic, monotonous buzz. But he couldn't bring himself to get up from the table opposite Morris James where they sat waiting for him to speak. Apart from the thud and buzz of the fly searching for light, and the the occasional awareness of a motor bike or lorry accelerating streets away, the silence grew oppressive. Morris James seemed to be in a state of shock and stared into space, seemingly unaware of his surroundings. Lambert glanced at his sergeant and sighed pointedly.

A big, solid, dependable man in his mid-thirties, Sergeant Tony Ellis looked like everyone's idea of a rugby playing Welshman. He had a jovial, avuncular face, broad flat nose, alert blue eyes and was losing his hair, which made him seem older than he was. Lambert, although only twelve years his senior, occasionally treated him like a surrogate son. It was something Ellis brought out in everyone. His parents had been killed in a car crash when he was in his late teens, and since that moment girls wanted to mother him and men tended to look after him. And he was equally caring and sensitive to the moods of others; he had an instinctive talent for understanding the most subtle and latent types of human behaviour and an ability to read the subtexts of most conversations. Now he became aware that Lambert was leaving the questioning to him. But for once he was at a loss, not knowing how to coax any information out of this pathetic little man who looked as if he should have been given medical help.

'Mr James,' he began tentatively. 'Do you feel well enough to tell us what happened?'

James looked confused. His eyes darted about the Interview Room, searching the bare walls for inspiration or help. His eyes came to rest on the uniformed constable standing near the door, and this seemed to reassure him for some reason.

'I couldn't stand it no more, so I killed her,' he told them, as if explaining something that was logical and simple.

Lambert exchanged a look with Ellis and said, 'After you'd been shopping, Mr James?'

Morris James frowned, trying to work it out.

'It's not a difficult question, Mr James,' prompted Ellis.

Lambert and Ellis waited in silence before springing

another question. They were both tacitly aware of how the silence could do their work for them, allowing it to settle in the impersonal atmosphere like motes of dust drifting slowly down the sunlight. And Ellis knew it was the way his boss liked to begin all his interrogations, pausing to savour the dramatic moment, letting the suspect think he was in for an easy ride.

Lambert studied James carefully. The man seemed to be burdened by an invisible yoke across his shoulders. He was wheezing asthmatically and there was a snail trail surrounding his paper-thin lips. He was ordinary to the point of transparency. His clothes looked as if they had been selected at random in charity shops: a grey shirt with blue checks, too tight under the arms, and a polyester, maroon tie with small grey diamonds.

'Did you murder your wife after you went shopping,' Lambert repeated quietly. 'Or was it before?'

James turned his head a fraction towards Lambert. 'Hmm?'

The detective raised the level of his voice. 'Did you murder your wife before or after you went shopping?'

'I think . . .' James began, then shook his head and lapsed into silence.

Lambert gave Sergeant Ellis a wearisome glance and Ellis took this as his cue to question the suspect again.

'Mr James? Did you kill your wife before or after you went to the supermarket?'

James stared at him for a moment before replying. 'I can't remember. I think it was before. What difference does it make? I killed her.'

'Did she put up a struggle?' Lambert cut in quickly.

'Struggle?'

'Yes. Did she put up a fight?'

James thought about it then nodded. Lambert glanced at the tape recorder.

'Is that a "yes", Mr James?'

'I suppose she must have done. I don't remember.'

Lambert caught Ellis's eye and shook his head. He put his finger on the tape recorder ready to switch off. 'Right. Interview suspended at 20.32 hours.'

James looked surprised. 'Is that it?' He seemed disappointed when he saw the tape being switched off.

'For the moment. There's someone I'd like you to talk to. Meanwhile, I'll get a cup of tea sent in to you.'

Lambert rose and left the interview room, followed by Ellis. Outside in the corridor, Ellis asked his superior, 'You don't suppose there's an outside chance he might have done it?'

Lambert laughed. 'Yeah. And Jeffrey Archer never lied.'

*   *   *

Evans arrived back at his flat and placed a bottle of Jack Daniel's he'd bought on the coffee table. He got a tumbler from the kitchen and poured himself a large measure. He switched his telephone back from divert then flopped onto the sofa and knocked back some of the whiskey. The back of his throat felt raw and the drink didn't help. He sat staring into space, willing himself to cry over his dead mother, but he felt numb. He took another sip of Jack Daniel's and a feeling of deep weariness washed over him. His eyes were drawn to the corner of the room where the guns lay hidden and it was a reminder. He had a job to do. He needed a clear head. If he woke tomorrow with a hangover, he might screw up.

He suddenly got to his feet, screwed the top back on the bottle, took it out into the kitchen and put it away in the food cupboard. Then he ran himself a tumbler of cold water from the tap and drank it. He returned to the living room, lay on his back on the floor, clasped his hands behind his neck and began to do sit-ups. The phone rang. He ignored it and continued with his exercises. After he reached twenty it stopped ringing, but soon after his mobile rang. He got up off the floor and switched it off completely.

'Sorry, Terry,' he said to himself. 'The answer's still no.'

*   *   *

As Sergeant Ellis followed Lambert into the office, he realised his cognitive powers of psychology were not about to be severely tested. Anyone with half a mind couldn't fail to notice the change that came over his superior when he saw the psychiatric nurse. She was standing at the window looking out onto the office block across the road and, like a car jamming on the brakes, Lambert stopped short as he entered, so that Ellis almost barged into him.

'Melanie Kokolios, psychiatric nurse,' she announced, turning to face them.

Ellis noticed her intelligent, warm, brown eyes, lighting up briefly when she saw Lambert; then cool instantly, like a light going out. She had thick, nut-brown hair, an aquiline nose and a slightly tanned complexion, and a figure that suggested regular work-outs at the gym.

'Hi, Melanie,' Lambert said. 'I thought you'd gone to live in New York.'

Ellis glanced at his boss, alert to the subtext that would inevitably follow as the attractive psychiatrist stared at Lambert, saying, 'As you can see, I'm back.'

'Permanently, I hope.'

Melanie Kokolios gave him a tiny shrug, pouting slightly. 'Maybe. Maybe not.'

Ellis was transfixed.

Lambert grinned and turned to Ellis. 'Her father's Greek.'

'And my mother's Welsh,' she told Ellis. Irritated by this pussy-footing around and determined to get down to business, her voice carried a slight edge.

28

Awkwardly, Ellis shifted slightly and said, 'Sounds like an interesting combination.'

Lambert caught the psychiatrist's eye. 'It is. Believe me, it is.'

Melanie Kokolios's response was hard and businesslike. 'So where's this false confession?'

'Sergeant Ellis'll show you. Like a coffee?' Before she could reply, Lambert dug into his pocket and handed the sergeant a coin. 'Get Mel a coffee, would you, sergeant?'

'How d'you like it?' Ellis asked her.

'Black no sugar,' Lambert replied.

Ellis threw his boss what his grandmother had always described as 'an old-fashioned look' before exiting. Melanie glared at Lambert, annoyed by the patronising, possessive way he had answered on her behalf, making it obvious to his colleague that they were once lovers.

Lambert gave her a puzzled, innocent expression. 'What's wrong?'

She ignored it. 'Give me a quick rundown on this false confession.'

'It's good to see you, Mel. It really is.' Lambert smiled tentatively. She continued to stare at him, eyes frosty. He sighed reluctantly before telling her, 'Wife an alcoholic. Looks like she was dried out but lapsed. He comes home with the weekly shop and finds her hanging from the bannisters.'

'And there's no way he could have done it?'

'No way.' Lambert frowned thoughtfully. 'Well, it's doubtful. Admittedly she probably weighed less than nine stone, but there was no sign of a struggle. I think she drank a bottle very quickly, got paralytic drunk and topped herself. I don't think she'd been dead long – maybe just a matter of minutes – when the husband found her. Perhaps she was still choking as he unpacked the shopping.'

The psychiatric nurse shuddered. Lambert thought about

putting a comforting arm round her but decided against it. Better not push his luck.

'Right,' she said, looking at her watch. 'I think I'd better . . .'

'Mel?' said Lambert. 'Do me a favour? I know this cosy little Italian restaurant . . .' He saw her mouth forming into an objection and continued hurriedly. 'I just want to know what's with the false confession, that's all. Call it professional interest. You can tell me all about it over a bottle of vino and some pasta.'

'If you're that interested, Harry, why don't you listen to the tape?'

'The tape won't give me your opinion, Mel,' he said, his expression sincere. 'And that's what I value.'

'Huh!' she exclaimed cynically.

'Honest. Shall we say tomorrow night? At seven?'

Chapter 3

Evans woke with a start and sat bolt upright. He knew it was a dream that had jolted him awake, but the dream had either vanished into the deeper recesses of his subconscious or been totally erased. He reached for his watch and saw that his body clock had let him down. It was gone eight-thirty. Usually he was awake every day at seven give or take ten minutes either side. This morning, for some reason, he had overslept, a thing that rarely happened to him. He'd slept for a solid ten hours, yet he felt more tired than usual, disoriented, as if he'd been drugged. He rubbed the sleep from his eyes then swung his legs out of bed. He glanced briefly and approvingly down at his nakedness, patting his firm stomach with the flat of his hand before striding into the bathroom. Refreshed by a cool shower, he shaved himself carefully, going over the same spot several times. He hated stubble. He liked the smoothness of a clean shave and didn't know how long it would be before his next shave.

Dress to kill, he thought as he flung open his wardrobe and selected a pair of paramilitary camouflage fatigues and a Dutch army shirt. Then he changed his mind, rejecting the military style in favour of a pair of dark-green jeans and a maroon sweatshirt. It was still effective camouflage but not so obvious.

After he had breakfasted on muesli, toast and strong black coffee, he fetched some of his mother's mementoes, which he kept in a chest of drawers in his bedroom, and stuffed them into a small holdall. There weren't many memories to dispose of, just a few postcards, letters and snapshots of them both together. And there was his favourite photograph of her. It had been taken before he was born,

31

when she was a beautiful young carnival queen riding on the float at the Tregaron Town Carnival. He put it into the bag with the other mementoes and returned to the living room, then dragged back the carpet covering his arms cache. He checked that the Browning had sufficient rounds before putting it into the holdall, along with an Ordnance Survey map of the area, a compass, box of matches and a torch. He then made himself a thermos flask of strong black coffee and put it into the bag with a packet of chocolate biscuits and some apples. The Armalite he disguised by wrapping several layers of carrier bags round it, then packed it inside a black bin liner. Finally, he checked that his mobile was charged up in case he needed to make a call, switched it to vibrate and clipped it to his belt.

Although it was late May, the summer had arrived early this year and the sun was threatening and overbearing, the sky cloudless and vivid blue. Apart from one short downpour, the last three weeks had been unusually hot and the newspapers had been full of paranoid features about global warming. Which was of no concern to Evans as he left his flat. He glanced up at the sky. He was hardened to whatever the elements chucked at him, but for once he was glad that he wouldn't have to lie around waiting to make the hit in the pouring rain. The heat he could cope with.

He put the holdall and Armalite in the boot of his black Sierra Cosgrove, instinctively glancing around to see if any neighbours were watching. Not that it mattered at this stage. A cod American voice drawled inside his head – 'A man's gotta do, what a man's gotta do' – a voice which belonged to his mate Terry. Evans endured this intrusion with an almost imperceptible smile, bordering on affection for his friend. In spite of Terry's cunning and deception, he reflected, he'd always been a reasonably good mate.

As he opened the car door, he stopped suddenly. An overwhelmingly powerful smell of milky ice-cream teased

32

and tricked him into believing he was near the seaside, reminding him of childhood days spent at the Mumbles with his mother; walks along the promenade, games in the park, sweets and ice-cream. He looked around to see if any children were walking by, eating ice-cream bought from the corner shop. But there was only the old man from the house opposite, walking his dog. Evans thought about the sweet fragrant smell, and how real it seemed. Then shrugged it off as a trick of the memory. After all, it wasn't so surprising. She'd been dead less than twenty-four hours now.

He drove with extreme caution through the town centre. He didn't want to get stopped for something trivial, which could result in a random search. It was no good taking risks at this stage of the game. Afterwards, it wouldn't matter. But now . . .

He drove north from Swansea, keeping within the speed limit. The sun burnt fiercely through the window on the right side of his face for most of the journey and he began to feel nauseous, but this could have been because of the anticipation of the kill as he got closer to his target. He sweated profusely, even though the air conditioning inside the car was effective. Twelve miles outside Swansea, as the car climbed up through Pontardawe towards the Black Mountain, he found the landmark he was looking for: the remote, decrepit looking pub called The Bull. Less than two hundred yards past the pub was the turning, an unmarked road, little more than a track, almost concealed by overgrown bramble bushes and sallow willow trees. He swung the car off the road and followed the track for about a mile, hoping he wouldn't meet anything coming the other way. And what if he met his target? What could he do? He'd have to shoot him at point blank range right here in the middle of the road. Like something out of a Tarantino film, violent and messy. No. He could well do without that. This had to be a good clean kill. From a distance. It was the only way.

The track rose at a steep angle and he changed into first gear. It was a gradient of about one in five and the direction changed, so that the sun at the top of the hill blinded him. He kept going, grabbing his sunglasses from under the windscreen. Once he had reached the brow of the hill, he saw the buildings below him. He braked and stopped, pausing to survey the farm. It was just what he'd expected. The farmhouse was dirty and insignificant, ramshackle and grey, as if covered with a layer of quarry dust. The hills surrounding the squalid smallholding seemed gloomy and threatening.

He eased the car into gear and let the clutch out slowly, allowing the car to cruise quietly down past the front of the farm. As he drove slowly by, he looked in through the broken gate which lay at an oblique angle with a rusting milk churn caught under it. He saw the name of the farm, lichen covered but still legible, scratched on a lump of slate set into the dry-stone wall by the entrance: Black Dog Farm.

He continued up the hill on the other side of this dark valley and drove until he could no longer see the farm in his rear view mirror. There was a narrow opening in the stone wall near the top of the hill and it was here the farm seemed to end, the land becoming more open, breaking out into mountainous terrain. He stopped the Sierra just past this opening, then reversed off the road, the wheels bumping over the stony track. But the ground was dry and firm, so there was no danger of getting stuck.

He took his holdall and the Armalite out of the boot and walked up the mountain away from the farm until he reached a small plateau, well out of sight of the road. He sat down, unzipped the bag and removed the photographs, letters and postcards. He spent a few minutes reading through each letter and card before piling them into a pyramid shape on a rock, then struck a match and set fire to the mound. He watched as the papers burned rapidly in the dry heat. A snapshot of him aged six, on a day trip to Barry Island, holding his mother's hand in front of the helter skelter, vanished in the flames.

Who had taken that photograph? Was it a stranger? Someone his mother had asked in passing? It wasn't his old man who had taken it, that was for sure. His father had never been on any outings or played with him. Never. Not once.

With a violent, sudden gesture, he threw the 10 x 8 onto the fire. It melted away quickly; one moment he was staring at his mother's beautiful young face, then in an instant she had disappeared. Ceased to exist.

He waited until the small fire had burnt itself out, making sure that not a single trace of paper was left, then rose and kicked the remains about with his feet, spreading the ashes far and wide over the rocky terrain. He picked up the bag and rifle, walked towards the rear of the farm and found a position looking down over the top of a corrugated roof outhouse or barn, offering a clear view of the entrance to the farmhouse which was at the side of the building. There was a flat rock he could lie on, hidden from the road by some brambles. And, significantly, the sun would be behind him for the rest of the day.

After he had unwrapped the Armalite, stuffing the carrier bags into the holdall, he lay on his stomach and watched and listened for any sounds coming from inside the farmhouse. It was just possible that his target had overslept and could emerge at any moment. But after another hour had passed, this seemed less likely. It was now just after eleven and getting hotter. The time stretched interminably. In the trees on the other side of the valley, crows broke the morning stillness with their ugly cries. In the decaying farmyard below, the skeleton of a tractor lay rusting among the weeds. Hens grumbled and pecked among the litter-strewn yard, picking their way through heaps of rotting debris. The occasional but sickening odour of manure drifted upwards and Evans cleared his throat and spat. Another hour crept agonisingly by. He was aware that the monotony was getting to him, so he listened to the sounds of the countryside, isolating and identifying them as he'd been trained to do in similar situations. He counted at least fifteen different sounds, everything from the distant barking of a dog to the close vibration of a small insect's wings. Another hour passed. Now he heard the sound of his stomach rumbling. He poured himself a coffee from the thermos and ate some chocolate biscuits. The chocolate melted quickly and made his fingers sticky and the cloying sweetness stuck in the back of his throat. He washed it down with a large gulp of coffee and his drowsiness soon began to disappear as the caffeine took effect. He closed one eye and peered along the barrel of the rifle, aiming it at head height on the door. From this distance he couldn't miss. Not with his training and experience.

By mid-afternoon there was still no sign of anyone returning to the farm. Evans sighed and looked at his watch for the umpteenth time. Just gone three. How much longer would he have to wait? He took an apple out of his bag, and had just taken a bite out of it when he heard the sudden roar and splutter of a vehicle coming over the hill and down the narrow road. He threw the apple to one side and took up his position.

It was a Land Rover, grey and ancient, down on one side as if the suspension was going. It was being driven erratically, the driver obviously worse for wear. It almost hit the gatepost as it turned into the farmyard, and screeched to a halt in front of the barn.

Evans's finger slid gently across the trigger.

He couldn't see the Land Rover now, it was tucked just under the corrugated barn. He heard the creaking hinges of the car door being opened, followed by a slam and a muttered oath. Suddenly the farmer lurched into view, staggering towards the farmhouse. Evans took careful aim. The farmer stopped to kick and curse at a hen that got in his way and almost lost his balance. He recovered, stood swaying for a moment, and continued towards the door.

Evans's finger tightened on the trigger. He was about to fire when the farmer stopped in the doorway and turned to look up towards the sky just above the barn, almost as if he could feel Evans's presence. The sun was in his eyes and he squinted. He was ruddy complexioned, from beer rather than a healthy outdoors existence. Evans studied the farmer's face carefully. It was the first time he had ever hesitated at a kill and he knew it was a costly mistake. The farmer suddenly fell in through the door and slammed it shut.

Evans couldn't believe his own stupidity. He was a professional killer, the best there was, and he'd blown it. Now what? He could either go down there and blow the farmer's brains out at point blank range, or wait for him to come out again. But judging by the state he was in, that could be some time.

Suddenly Evans felt a tingling sensation at his hip. His mobile. He unclipped it from his belt and checked the display. It was Terry calling him.

He clicked the answer button. No harm in seeing what Terry wanted. After all, he was a mate. And he could do with a friend at a time like this.

Chapter 4

Like a cocky young teenager, Lambert grinned across the table at Melanie as they sat down. She stared back at him with feigned indifference, wondering why on earth she had agreed to have dinner with him. Perhaps it was just curiosity, pure and simple. She couldn't think of any other reason.

The short, tubby proprietor bounded over to their table and greeted them effusively. 'How are you, sir? A long time no see, huh? And you, madam. How are you both keeping?'

'Very well thank you, Angelo,' said Lambert. 'We've both been out of town for a while, but it's good to be back.'

The proprietor beamed at them. 'Ah yes. There's no place like home. No?'

Lambert winced at the choice of words, wondering if it was deliberate. He stared directly into the restaurateur's eyes, searching for any hidden meaning. But Angelo's eyes, he remembered, always had a mischievous twinkle for all his customers. Lambert smiled at him.

'Be careful, Angelo. You might end up in Kansas.'

Angelo made a questioning, comic opera face.

'*The Wizard of Oz*,' Lambert explained. 'Dorothy.'

'Ah yes,' Angelo said, though it was obvious he hadn't a clue what Lambert was on about. 'Now then – can I get you a drink?'

'I think we'll get straight onto the wine. OK for you, Mel?'

Melanie gave a cursory nod. The proprietor handed Lambert the wine list but he waved it aside. 'A bottle of Chianti Rufina. Thanks.'

As he went to get the wine, Lambert looked round the restaurant, remembering some of their clandestine dinners.

He caught Melanie's eye. She was staring at him intently, waiting for him to speak. He felt suddenly awkward. And he felt a sharp stab of guilt as he was reminded of all the lies and complications their affair had spawned. After it was over, and Melanie had gone to live in New York, Helen had one day suggested she would like to eat at this restaurant. He had made a feeble excuse, saying he didn't fancy Italian food on that particular evening; but when she repeated the request weeks later, he told her some colleagues from work had eaten here and had come down with food poisoning. Lying to Helen led to the slander of Angelo's. Double the remorse.

'Have you ever gone back,' said Melanie, 'to a place you knew from years ago?'

'I hear what you're saying, Mel. But it's good to be back here. With you. Just like old times.'

'With a slight difference. We don't have to keep looking over our shoulders.'

'How did you know Helen and I had split up?'

'I heard.'

'News travels fast round here. I expect you heard about my old man, as well.'

Melanie shook her head and waited for him to explain. She could tell by his serious expression what was coming.

'Massive heart attack last Thursday.'

'Did he . . .' She hesitated, wondering whether the occasion demanded a euphemism.

'Funeral was yesterday,' said Lambert, raising his eyebrows and making a palms-up, apologetic gesture, as if father's death was beyond his control.

Angelo returned with the Chianti and held the bottle for Lambert's approval. With barely a glance at it, the detective nodded, keeping his eyes on Melanie.

After the proprietor had poured the wine, given them both menus and gone, Lambert clinked glasses with Melanie's.

'Iechyd da!'

'Yamas!' she said, instantly regretting the Greek reply. That's how it had been when they were lovers.

Lambert grinned confidently at her. '*Just* like old times.'

She didn't believe for an instant he wanted to know about the false confession. He was trying to rekindle their relationship; she could tell by his body language, every little gesture. When they arrived at the restaurant she had felt his touch as he held the door open for her, his hand brushing the small of her back, then slightly lower.

'You don't waste much time in mourning, do you,' she said. 'I thought you and your dad were very close.'

'We were alike. So I've been told. But it was more of an accusation.'

*   *   *

Ted Wilson opened his eyes and tried to focus on something. Anything. Eventually the corner of the mantlepiece swam into view and he knew where he was, slumped in the armchair in front of the fireplace that still contained the charred remains of some wooden pallets he had burnt last February when he ran out of coal. His mouth felt rancid and his bladder pained him. He realised he was dying for a piss. That was a bit of luck, waking just in time. About a month ago, he'd got drunk on market day and come home in this condition. He'd gone to bed and slept through to the middle of the night, and was awakened by a very real dream. He dreamt he was standing in the pub toilet, unzipping his flies, taking his cock out and pissing. The sheer relief was unbelievable. That's when he woke to discover he had emptied his very full bladder in bed. Thank Christ he had woken in time now. He couldn't have been as pissed as he thought.

He rose unsteadily from the chair. He knew that if he didn't relieve himself pretty quickly he'd have another accident. Wheezing and spluttering, he staggered towards the door and grabbed the handle. It was still fairly light outside, the sun an ominous fireball hanging over the horizon. He shuffled along the wall of the house, turned inwards, unzipped himself and let out a stream. He watched his urine splashing against the wall, hot and steaming. It was physically satisfying, this sheer relief of letting go.

It was his final gratification.

The bullet entered the back of his head at a downward angle, passed through the centre of his skull, scattering his brains and face across the brick wall, as his body smashed against the side of the house with the powerful impact. He didn't hear the sound of the shot. He was dead before it reached him.

A family of crows, frightened by the noise, scattered from a nearby tree.

*　　　　　*　　　　　*

Lambert paused in his meal, taking pleasure in watching Melanie as she meticulously dissected her grilled trout. She looked up and caught the sentimental look in his eyes.

'What?' she demanded with a trace of irritation.

'I've missed you, Mel. Every time I think about you . . .'

'I thought you wanted to talk about the false confession.'

'I do. But being here with you . . .'

She interrupted him again. 'Reminds you of our sordid little affair.' She saw him wince, giving her a wounded expression. Or was he just playing the hurt little boy again? She didn't trust that sincere look of his.

'Come on, sweetheart. It wasn't like that.'

'No?'

'No. Well, not for me it wasn't. OK, admittedly we might not always have had the opportunity to make love in conventional places . . .'

41

'I thought that was part of the attraction for you, Harry.'

'Well, maybe to begin with, but . . .'

'Oh, you mean you got bored doing it in the back of your passion wagon? And here was I thinking you found it exciting.'

He shifted uncomfortably in his seat. Good. She might have succeeded in rattling his composure, shaken his self-confidence. He was always so sure of himself. She was reminded of the first time they met. She worked at the hospital and when he almost collided with her in the corridor just outside her office, he did a very obvious double-take, which at the time she found funny and flattering. She could clearly remember his opening gambit.

'Do you believe in love at first sight?'

She remembered blushing, and stammering, 'There's no such thing.'

'I didn't think so either,' he countered. 'Up until now.'

It was as corny as a cracker joke. But she fell for it. Not immediately. But he was persistent and eventually managed to wear down her resistance with outrageous flattery, charm and perseverence. God! What an idiot she'd been. And here she was: sitting in the restaurant where they'd had their first date. She needed to have her brains tested. Some psychiatrist.

Angelo returned to their table, topped up their wine glasses and asked them if everything was to their satisfaction.

'Put it this way,' said Melanie. 'The food and the service are excellent.'

Angelo sensed the sudden drop in temperature, and gave them a small nod and a half smile before turning away.

'Listen, Mel,' said Lambert. 'I always found our lovemaking exciting, wherever it was. It's just that . . . well, I wanted our relationship to go deeper than . . . er . . .'

'A quick shag?'

'It was difficult at the time. What with Natasha studying for her A Levels.'

Melanie sighed deeply and shook her head. 'You know your trouble, don't you?'

'Come on then, doc: hit me with the prognosis.'

'It's boringly common. It's called having your cake and eating it.'

His confidence returning, Lambert smiled. 'Stupid expression.'

'So d'you want to hear about the false confession or not?'

'It's why we're here.'

Melanie felt her mouth being tugged into a lopsided, cynical smile, which she tried to suppress but failed.

*   *   *

The sun had almost vanished over the hills. Soon it would be pitch black.

Evans stood over the corpse, forcing himself to stare at the sordid mess. He was testing himself, to see if there were any feelings of remorse that might surface from deep inside him. But he felt nothing at all. His emotions had been blunted by the repeated bloodshed of previous jobs.

He was startled suddenly by the sound of a vehicle, the accelerator being revved hard as it climbed the steep hill on the road leading to the farm. He turned and ran, out into the road and up towards where his Sierra was parked, away from the approaching vehicle. He sat in his car and waited, listening.

*   *   *

'So,' said Lambert, pushing the last of his lasagna to the side of his plate. 'Why *did* poor old Morris James confess?'

Melanie took a sip of wine before launching into the explanation.

'Because years ago his wife fell in love with his brother Richard.'

'Was this before she and Morris got together? Or after?'

'Before. I don't think Sadie was remotely interested in dull-as-ditchwater Morris.'

'Sadie and Morris, eh.' Lambert laughed. 'What a double act.'

'D'you want to hear this or not?'

'Go on.'

'Anyway, Richard falls in love with someone else. They marry and settle in Australia. And Sadie settles for second best, hoping to find some reflection of her lover in his brother. But Morris was a big disappointment. Nothing like his dynamic brother.'

Parodying amazement, Lambert let his mouth drop open. 'Morris had a *dynamic* brother?'

'It's possible. And as Morris's relationship with Sadie gets worse, his self-esteem takes a nose dive. Then, when Richard suddenly kicks the bucket down under, Sadie takes to the bottle. Morris carries on as normal, but deep down he hates his wife, and he'd like to kill her. He plots her death a million times, this pathetic man. Then, when she obliges by doing it for him, he feels guilty, thinks he really has murdered her.'

'Families,' said Lambert. 'The things we do to one another.'

*   *   *

Evans heard the car stop outside the farm, followed by a door slamming shut. Any second now someone would discover the corpse. He turned the ignition, threw the car into gear and accelerated. The car shot forward, bumping over the uneven ground, the tyres squealing as it rounded the corner into the narrow road. As he sped down the hill, hoping there was enough room to pass the other car, he switched his headlights on. He could see the other car now. It looked like a Fiat Panda, so there might be enough room to squeeze past. But only just. With his offside scratching along the hedgerow, he pushed hard on the accelerator and scraped passed the Fiat. But his wing mirror must have caught it and there was a crash as it was wrenched off into the road.

'Fuck!' he shouted over the noise. But he kept his foot hard on the accelerator as he climbed the hill. When he reached the top he checked his mirror to see if the farm visitor had run out into the road, trying to get his registration number. All he saw was the blackness of the valley behind him. Night had descended.

*   *   *

After Angelo had cleared their plates, Lambert looked searchingly at Melanie. 'Can I ask you something?'

'You can ask. But I can't guarantee I'll give you an answer.'

'Well, I think Helen's going for a divorce.'

Melanie leaned back in her chair and eyed him suspiciously. She guessed what was coming. He was so predictable. She managed to restrain the amused smile she could feel quivering at the corners of her mouth.

'So? What's that got to do with me? I've not been around for two years. You can't blame me for splitting up the marriage. There's probably been someone else on the scene since then.'

'That's not what I meant.'

'What then?'

Suddenly Lambert felt unsure of himself.

'We could always get it together again.'

'Smooth talker.'

'I've got my own flat out on the Mumbles. It's . . . well, it's okay I suppose. At least it's got a sea view.'

Melanie widened her eyes in mock surprise.

'Wow! This is so romantic and unexpected. How could any woman resist?'

'And I don't want to be on my own. Not tonight. Not after burying the old man yesterday.'

Melanie's eyes narrowed. 'Moral blackmail. You'd stoop that low?'

Lambert gave her his most charming smile. 'You know me.'

'So let me get this straight – you want us to pick up where we left off after a gap of nearly two years?'

'I love that look in your eyes. So warm and sexy.'

'Come on, Harry: is that the best you can do?'

Lambert shrugged and smiled. 'Well, I just thought . . .'

'You've got no chance, inspector.'

He had known that from the start of the evening. But somehow he felt a compulsion to flirt with her in the most outrageous way. It was because he knew that it was a lost cause that he could be as unsubtle and as obvious as he liked.

'Out of all the men in Swansea,' Melanie added, 'you would be bottom of my list.'

Lambert grinned. 'Don't spare my feelings, Mel. Just tell me straight.'

'You're a bloody misogynist. Oh, I know you once told me you're in love with all women. But you're mistaken . . .'

He raised his eyes towards the ceiling. 'Is this a free analysis?'

She found his complacency and flippancy irritating, and her voice rose a trace. 'You seem to be hell-bent on destroying women. Jack the Ripper without a knife. For knife read penis.'

Lambert was tempted to mock her with the term psychobabble, thought better of it, and said, 'Each man kills the thing he loves.'

She raised her eyebrows in mock surprise. 'Oscar Wilde. You surprise me.'

'Don't be patronising, Mel. I have got a bit more culture than the odd Chuck Norris video.'

'Who?'

'You've never heard of . . .' He tutted amazement. 'Your lack of street cred is showing.'

She poked her tongue out at him. He laughed, and could see that she felt more relaxed in his company now. He thought about reaching across the table and placing his hand on hers, but the thought was interrupted by his mobile ringing. Although it was in his inside pocket, it was still shrill enough to pierce the restaurant ambience.

'Sorry,' he said, 'but you know what it's like.'

'How could I forget,' she sighed, casting her eyes round at the other diners, who seemed to be looking at her with a mixture of pity and disbelief.

'Harry here,' Lambert announced into the mobile. He listened carefully, his face becoming serious and businesslike. This, thought Melanie, was the other side of the coin. No more flirting. No more chat up. It was down to business now. And she wondered which was more important to him, the philandering or his work. She decided they were on about an equal footing.

'OK, Tony,' he said. 'I'll be there right away.'

He switched the phone off and paused, taking a moment to show her how apologetic he was. 'I'm sorry, Mel. I have to go. Let's continue this another time.' He waved at the proprietor. 'Angelo! Could we have the bill, please?' As he reached for his wallet, he told her, 'I'll give you a bell.'

'Don't bother,' she said, rising. 'I won't be in.'

Lambert looked genuinely surprised and hurt. She looked across the table that divided them and threw him an apologetic half-hearted smile, like a consolation prize.

'Harry, you had two chances of us getting together again. Slim and none.'

In spite of his sense of failure, Lambert laughed. 'I'll go for the former,' he said. 'And live in hope.'

Chapter 5

As he drove out of Swansea, Lambert thought about Melanie's parting kiss. It had been gentle, full on the lips, which he found disconcerting after what she had said. Perhaps she was curious, wanting to see how she felt towards him physically. He had wanted to prolong the kiss but, just as he was about to reach out to hold her tight, she pulled away, turned and walked off. He stood watching until she was out of sight, admiring the alluring sway of her hips, waiting to see if she looked back over her shoulder. Had she glanced back, he might have been in with a chance, however remote. But she kept walking without turning round. So that was that.

The headlights of an approaching car flashed angrily, reminding him to dip his headlights. 'Sorry, mate,' he said, as if the other driver could hear him, and switched his main beam onto dip.

He followed Tony Ellis's directions and found The Bull without much difficulty, but then missed the narrow turning and had to reverse back for fifty yards. As he climbed the steep hill, his headlights on full beam, the overhanging trees on either side of the narrow road appeared threatening, a tunnel of gnarled and ghostly branches. It was the perfect setting for murder. Even though he'd seen some gruesome sights in his time, as he neared the scene of a crime, Lambert felt a queasiness in his stomach. It was always the same. The anticipation was worse than the event. Once he was at the scene he was able to get on with the job and not allow his feelings to get in the way. He could switch off his emotions and take control. Except for that time, about three years ago. She'd been only six years old and the victim of the most horrendous rape and assault. Images of her frail and vulnerable body still haunted him at nights. At the time,

48

most of his team had needed counselling to deal with their feelings. Lambert had turned to Helen, wept like a baby in her arms. She had supported him, eased the pain, nursed him back from the horror of what he'd seen, and loved him. Loved him! God! What an idiot he'd been, discarding her love like a worn carpet.

His hands tightened on the wheel as he reached the brow of the hill. Above and before him stretched the vast night sky, a dark, velvet cloth sprinkled with sparkling silver like hundreds-and-thousands.

He eased the car gently over the stony track. As he started the descent into the valley below, he could see the glow of the halogen lights at the murder scene, making it appear unreal, like a night shoot on a film location. As he neared the farm, he saw the congestion of police vehicles in the narrow lane, so he parked his car about a hundred yards up the lane and walked the rest of the way. He was met by Sergeant Ellis at the farm gate, his face glowing red and his forehead glistening with perspiration.

'Tony,' Lambert acknowledged with a nod. 'How long have SOCO been here?'

'A good hour.'

Having donned a pair of overshoes from one of the SOCO vans, they walked towards the cordoned-off section of the farmyard, past flashing blue lights and policemen in white coveralls searching the area for evidence. One of the officers took their details and checked them in. But before they reached the cordon, Lambert stopped suddenly, as if reluctant to visit the crime scene.

'What's the story so far, Tony?'

Indicating the murder scene with a tilt of the head, Ellis replied, 'The victim's an old boy called Ted Wilson.'

'Is he the owner of this dump?'

Ellis nodded. 'But he didn't do much farming, by all accounts. Piss artist from way back, he was.'

'How d'you know this?'

'Chap who found him told us. Bloke by the name of Tom Jones. Not the singer.'

Lambert stared impassively at him.

'Yes, well,' the sergeant continued, 'Mr Jones was on his way round to collect a debt.'

'And he doesn't get his money so he kills the bugger?'

'For fifty quid? When I phoned you, I said the victim was shot, didn't I?'

'So? Most of these farmers own shotguns.'

Ellis shook his head. 'This was no shotgun. It was a high-power rifle. And it appears that Wilson was shot from a distance. From somewhere over there. Around seventy-five yards at a rough guess.'

They continued towards the murder scene, ducking under the police tape, and met the SOCO officer in charge.

'Hello, Hughie,' Lambert greeted him. 'What you got for me this time?'

The officer, round-faced and double-chinned, his eyes glinting, pursed his lips and shook his head. 'D'you wanna take a butchers? It's not a pretty sight.'

'I can live without it. I've just had a lasagna.'

In spite of his reluctance to see the bloody mess, Lambert forced himself to look down at the corpse.

'Brains and face spattered all over the bloody wall,' said Hughie with undisguised relish.

Lambert wondered whether it was because Hughie was a bloodthirsty little sod, or whether he enjoyed seeing his fellow officers squirm. Whatever the reason, he seemed to have a passion for grisly crimes, the more gruesome the better. It was his world. His *raison d'être*. And he loved it.

Lambert's expression gave nothing away when he saw the farmer's exposed penis. He turned to Hughie. 'What about his tackle?'

The officer smirked. 'Nothing pervy about it. Guy was

taking a piss. Bang. The lights go out. Is nothing sacred any more?'

'Sergeant Ellis tells me he was shot with a high-powered rifle.'

'Yeah. Strange that. It looks like a professional job. Whoever did this was a marksman.'

'Could have been a nutter from a gun club.'

'There is that.'

'Where's the bloke who found him?'

Hughie nodded in the direction of one of the vehicles. 'With DC Maynard.'

Lambert glanced over towards the far side of the farmyard, where he saw a middle-aged man in track suit bottoms, wellington boots and a check shirt, leaning against a patrol car and being handed a disposable cup from DC Maynard. Lambert noticed Maynard was wearing her tight black trousers again. Because she always seemed to wear the same thing, dirty jokes and speculation about Maynard's lack of hygiene in the nether regions had gone round the station among Lambert's male colleagues. Though Lambert, perhaps because he found Maynard strangely attractive with her snub nose, rather pugnacious jaw, but mysterious aquamarine eyes, gave her the benefit of the doubt, and liked to believe she had several pairs of identical trousers.

As he started to walk over, Hughie said, 'You haven't asked me what I've got in my little plastic bag here.'

Lambert stopped and turned back. Hughie was holding up the bag containing what looked like an apple.

'Could have been the killer's lunch or tea,' Hughie explained. 'Found it on the hill up there, just behind the barn. Looks like he took one bite out of it, then chucked it.'

'Good. Even if forensic don't get a good pattern, there'll be some saliva on it. Thanks, Hughie. Keep up the good work.'

'Yeah, see you in a bit.'

Ellis at his side, Lambert continued towards DC Maynard and the witness. As he got close to them, he noticed the man had a red nose and cheeks, but the area round his eyes was white, as if sunglasses were worn regularly, although Lambert suspected it was more likely to be a skin condition caused by excessive alcohol. If Lambert was asked to guess what he did for a living, farmer would be the obvious choice.

'Mr Jones?' he said. 'Detective Inspector Lambert. You found the body, I believe.'

Mr Jones sniffed and pulled at his nose with an oil-stained finger and thumb before replying. 'Aye. Fifty fucking quid he owed me.'

'You can kiss that goodbye.'

'Don't I know it. Owed every bugger money, he did. Not a lot. Fiver here – tenner there. But fifty! Never should've lent it him.'

'So why did you?'

Jones grinned sheepishly. 'Pissed, weren't I. And the crafty fucker . , .' He checked himself and turned towards DC Maynard. ''Scuse my French, miss.'

DC Maynard's eyes blinked several times and she nodded non-committally.

'Go on,' Lambert prompted the farmer. 'You were explaining why you agreed to lend him fifty pounds.'

'Oh yes, well, he gives me a cock and bull story about how he'd won the lottery – five numbers, like. Huh!' He paused and slurped his tea noisily. 'Reckoned he had a few grand due.'

Ellis, wondering why Lambert seemed so intent on pursuing what seemed to be a fairly irrelevant line of questioning, said, 'Mr Jones reckons he spotted the killer's car.'

Lambert stared at the witness. 'Oh?'

'Black it was.'

'And the make?'

'Ain't got a clue. Cars is not my strong point.'

Ellis exchanged a disappointed look with Lambert, which Jones appeared not to notice as he began to relive the scene.

'Some of these buggers drive like lunatics. On my way here, on the main road just before The Bull, there's a sharp corner, and I nearly hit one of them fancy four wheel drive fuckers.' He looked contritely at DC Maynard and started to apologise again.

'Don't worry,' she told him. 'Pretend I'm not here.'

'Yes, well,' continued the farmer, 'nearly hit the bastard. Shook me up it did, I can tell you. Then when I pulled in here . . .'

He broke off as the memory of discovering the corpse hit him.

'You found Wilson?' Lambert said with a little more urgency.

'I thought I was going to throw up. That's when I heard this car starting up – just up the road there. He drove right past the gate, going like the clappers. Smashed my fucking wing mirror.'

This time, having decided the occasion excused the use of bad language, Jones avoided looking at DC Maynard.

'D'you manage to get a look at him?'

'It was getting dark. And he was going too quick. It all happened so sudden like.'

'But you could see it was a man?'

'Oh, it was a bloke all right. I could see his shadow, like. Young bloke, I think it was. With short hair.'

'What I'd like to do, Mr Jones,' said Lambert, with a sideways glance at DC Maynard, 'is to get you a book of makes and models of cars, to see if you can pick one out for us.'

'Well, I'll try. But the way these buggers drive round here, he could be halfway to John O'Groats by now.'

'Maybe,' said Lambert thoughtfully. 'Maybe not.'

This wasn't lost on Ellis, who recognised Melanie Kokolios's influence on his boss's reply.

*   *   *

Evans switched on the interior light, took a pen torch from the glove compartment and studied the Ordnance Survey map for a while. He had to hurry, in case someone decided to pull in and park behind him in the lay-by. A heavy lorry thundered past and the car shook in the draught. He peered through the window on the passenger side. There was a half moon tonight, giving just enough light for him to see the ivy covered trunk of an enormous oak tree in a field on the other side of the fence. This was as good enough a place as any. But would he be able to find it again? He took another look at the map, memorising the landmarks in the immediate area, then took the Browning from the holdall and wrapped it in a plastic bag. He could bury it in the field, near the oak tree, just the other side of the fence.

*   *   *

'What a shithole,' Ellis said as they searched the squalid farmhouse. 'Stinks too.'

Lambert opened a wartime utility sideboard, one leg broken, and rooted through the contents, finding empty beer bottles, crisp packets, a copy of *Penthouse*, some blue and white china that might have been worth something once but was badly chipped and cracked, and an old rusting biscuit tin containing an assortment of nails and screws.

'Just junk,' he declared. 'Filthy bloody junk. And what does that tell you about the victim, other than the fact that bluebottles found him attractive?'

Ellis stopped searching for a moment and shrugged.

'Nothing. Wilson may have had a roof over his head but he lived like a vagrant.'

'It's incredible,' Lambert agreed. 'There's not a single shred of evidence that indicates he had a past. No photos, no ornaments, nothing. But, according to old Tom Jones, he lived here for thirty odd years.'

Ellis found an old coal scuttle used as a waste bin, overflowing with paper and tin foil cartons. 'Yeah, and had Chinese takeaways and fish and chips every day of it.'

Underneath a bundle of old newspapers, mostly copies of *The Sun* and *Sunday Sport*, Lambert found a small coronet.

'Take a look at this.'

'What is it?'

'Some sort of crown, the kind children dress up in. Must be quite old. Look how rusty the metal is.'

Ellis sighed with frustration. 'A bit of Wilson's history? Or just more rubbish?'

'No, the rest is rubbish. This is junk as in bric à brac.'

DC Maynard entered hurriedly, breathless with excitement.

'Sir, Jones thinks the man may have been driving a Sierra.'

Lambert slammed the coronet onto the sideboard. 'Right! Get onto records. There can't be that many black Sierras in . . .'

Maynard interrupted him, looking pleased with herself. 'I've already done it. Apparently there's less than two dozen in the Swansea area.' She handed him a handwritten list. 'Have a look at number ten on the list.'

Lambert read it aloud. 'A black Sierra Cosgrove, registered in the name of G. Evans. Ex-paratrooper and SAS.'

'I ran the list by Criminal Records and they came up with his name. He was charged with GBH when he was a young squaddie. The sentence was suspended.'

Lambert stared at Ellis. 'It's got to be him.'

55

Chapter 6

Evans poured himself a large Jack Daniel's and took a sip. The drink felt good, warm and soothing. Now that it was almost over, he could relax. His eyes darted to the Armalite beside him on the sofa. He pictured the bloody corpse of the farmer, brains and blood spattered across the wall of that disgusting farmhouse, and he thought about his feelings, probing inside his mind for the slightest hint of an emotion. There was nothing but a vast emptiness, a cavernous silence inside his head. Unthinkingly, he patted the Armalite's stock, as if it was a sweet child to be congratulated for a job well done, and listened to the night-time sounds of the flat; the mechanical hum of the fridge and the creaking and shifting of the fabric of the building as it expanded and contracted in the changing temperature of the coming dawn.

An image flew into his head suddenly: an omnipotent, giant Lottery finger pointing down accusingly at a pathetic cowering figure and blowing out his brains.

Evans blinked hard, chasing away the sudden urge to close his eyes and drift into sleep. He checked his watch, got up off the sofa and stood the Armalite against the wall in the far corner of the room.

It was down to business again.

He moved quickly back to the sofa, picked up the phone and dialled the number of the First Direct Bank. As soon as his security code had been cleared, he gave his instructions in a clear, businesslike manner.

'I'd like to transfer fifteen thousand pounds from my account.'

*   *   *

Keeping low behind a row of parked cars, DC Maynard moved stealthily back up the street to where Lambert stood waiting with the uniformed chief superintendent.

'Well?' demanded Lambert.

She nodded seriously. 'This has got to be it. Wing mirror's broken off on the driver's side. And the car's covered in a film of chalky dust.'

Lambert turned towards the chief super at his side. 'It's our man all right.'

Chief Superintendent Phillips checked his watch. 'Less than an hour till it's light. I'll give it another forty-five minutes. We'll hit our target just before dawn.'

Lambert smiled to himself. He knew Phillips loved all the Hollywood-style hard man talk. He made eye contact with DC Maynard and could see she was thinking the same.

'On the other hand,' Phillips muttered, thinking aloud, 'there's no real reason why we shouldn't get it over and done with.'

'I quite agree, sir,' said Lambert. 'Now's a good a time as any.'

With an extravagant gesture, Phillips checked his watch again and spoke in a clipped, efficient tone. 'Let's say five minutes from now. We hit him good and hard. I'll go and tell the men.'

Abruptly, Phillips wheeled about in a military fashion and marched towards some unmarked police vehicles.

'D'you think he'll put up any resistance, sir?' DC Maynard asked Lambert.

'I wouldn't like to speculate,' he replied non-committally. 'But we know he's armed and we can't take that chance.'

DC Maynard smiled warmly, looking him straight in the eyes. It was, he realised, manipulative. He was aware that she was using her sex, but for what purpose he was uncertain. Perhaps she fancied him. Or she could have been fishing for some well-deserved compliments. He sensed that she was ambitious, so maybe that was it. He returned her smile and caught himself saying,

'Well done, Carol. Good work tonight.'

'Thank you, sir,' she whispered, dropping her eyes demurely, deliberately letting him see the softer side of her character.

With any other woman, Lambert would have made his move now. But his golden rule was not with anyone in the service. Only civilians. It was bad enough having a reputation as a middle-aged Lothario without shitting on your own doorstep. He was relieved when Ellis came tearing back from using the car phone because he just might have been tempted.

'It doesn't look good,' Ellis announced. 'They eventually let me speak to Evans's old commanding officer. He was none too pleased at being woken at the crack.'

'Tough shit. What did he say?'

Ellis looked up towards Evans's first floor flat, an expression of deep concern spread across his face. 'This is one hell of a dangerous bloke. Trained to kill. No longer in the SAS. He now sells his services to anyone who needs a freelance soldier.'

'Christ! An armed mercenary from the SAS. What are we getting into here?'

Phillips arrived back and overheard Lambert's last remark. 'What's that?' he demanded. Lambert told him about Ellis's phone call to SAS Headquarters at Hereford, and he said, 'This is fucking armed combat. The SAS should do their own dirty work.'

Ellis laughed ironically. 'I got the impression they'd like to disown him, sir.'

Phillips gritted his teeth and tugged at his leather gloves. 'I bet they would,' he said. 'Right! Let's go for it.'

*   *   *

58

Evans poured himself another slug of whiskey and looked at his watch. Not long now until daylight. If they were going to come it would be any minute now. He knew that the optimum time for a raid was just before dawn, when the target is probably fast asleep and at his lowest ebb, especially if he's had a bad night and just dropped off to sleep.

The only light coming into the living room was through the open door leading to the kitchen. He got up from the sofa, switched it off, then walked over to the window. Slowly and carefully he eased the curtain back a fraction. The street looked quiet and empty, the incandescent light from the street lamps shaping it into a uniformly unreal and sepia-tinted scene. The before-dawn-quiet buzzed in his head. He kept watching but there seemed to be no one out there. Perhaps he had overestimated their capabilities. Supposing no one came. What then?

A dark shape moved between two parked cars. Had he imagined it? He kept staring at the cars, concentrating. Then he saw the shadow emerge from its hiding place, solid and real, and unmistakably wearing a blue uniform. They were here all right. Any second now. He let the curtain fall back into place, switched the light on again in the kitchen and returned to the sofa. He leaned back, stretching his legs out in front of him, took another gulp of Jack Daniel's and waited.

*　　　　　*　　　　　*

'Shit!' hissed Phillips as the static of his walkie talkie crackled. He fiddled with the volume control and commanded, 'OK. This is it. Don't take any chances. No heroes. Understood? OK. Go! Go!'

Lambert, Ellis and Maynard prepared to follow close behind Phillips. Across the street, immediately opposite the target's flat, a man in a baseball cap and a backpack over one shoulder prepared to leave for work. He stopped in his tracks as the tearing sound of splintering wood disturbed the early morning calm. He watched open-mouthed the sledge-hammering of the door and saw the first wave of police officers breaking into the house.

'Get him out of the immediate area, Carol,' Lambert shouted over the din. 'Quick as you can.'

Disappointed she would no longer be part of the raid, DC Maynard hesitated, 'Yes, but . . .'

'Now!' yelled Lambert, then turned his back on her and followed Ellis and Phillips into the house. He stepped over the broken door, following closely behind Ellis, who was about to take the stairs two at a time when the door of the ground floor flat opened a fraction and a pale frightened face stared out through the crack.

'Sergeant!' Lambert yelled.

Ellis didn't need to be told twice. He turned at the stairs, took his ID out of his back pocket, and ran towards the ground floor flat, saying, 'It's OK, sir. Police officers. Everything's under control. Get back inside.'

Lambert heard the crash of Evans's door being forced open as he raced up the stairs. He arrived on the landing as three armed officers leapt inside, brandishing their rifles, screaming and shouting, 'Freeze! Hold it! Don't move! I've got him. I've got him.'

Lambert followed Phillips through the door. He held his breath against the clouds of dust and smell of fear. The three armed officers were frozen like statues, their rifles trained on Evans, just the right pressure on the trigger, hardly daring to breathe. A deathly silence. They eased their fingers off the triggers and one of them looked towards the chief superintendent, as if he needed some sort of reassurance or explanation. Phillips and Lambert stared at the professional killer for what seemed like an eternity. Evans smiled confidently at them and sipped his whiskey.

'You only had to ring the doorbell,' he said, 'and I'd have let you in.'

Chapter 7

Lambert knew Evans was about to confess. He could sense it. He had seen so many suspects in similar situations. They either dug in their heels and denied it, in which case you were in for a long-drawn-out battle of wits, or else they confessed almost immediately, glad that it was all over.

Evans took a deep breath before speaking. 'Yes, I shot him. But that's all I'm saying. I killed him, an' that's that.'

Brief looks were exchanged between Lambert, Ellis and Maynard. The solicitor, who appeared to be present merely as a formality, studied his fingernails and remained silent.

'What was your motive, Mr Evans?' Lambert asked, his voice subdued and low, like a priest in the confessional, not wanting to disturb the mood of the confessor.

Evans stared straight ahead, his eyes distant.

'I repeat: "What was your motive, Mr Evans?"'

Evans's eyes didn't flicker. He continued staring into the distance.

Lambert's voice took on a sharper edge. 'How did you know Ted Wilson?'

'Did you have a reason to kill him?' Ellis asked. 'Why, Mr Evans? Why? What was the reason? We have to know.'

Silence. The silence stretched to breaking point. DC Maynard watched Evans intently, staring hard into his eyes, watching for any signs that he might be faking the trance-like state into which he seemed to have retreated. Outwardly, Lambert gave the appearance of being in control. No one could guess how frustrated he felt. It was an easy confession; too easy. Something told him that this was all they would get out of Evans. Instinct told him that Evans meant it about not saying another word. But he decided to give it one last try.

'No rational person kills without reason, Mr Evans. Was this a contract killing? Did someone pay you to kill Ted Wilson?'

Evans continued to stare lifelessly into space. Lambert looked questioningly at the solicitor, who shrugged then shook his head.

'Right. Interview suspended at 10.05 hours.' Lambert clicked the tape off and got up from the table. He studied Evans carefully before he spoke. 'I think I'll take a trip to Hereford and have a word with your old CO.'

Evans's eyes flickered slightly.

'Oh?' said Lambert. 'You're hearing's not impaired then?'

He turned and strode out of the interview room.

*   *   *

After the cell door clanged shut, Evans thought he was probably being observed through the aperture, so he continued staring into space for a long time. As soon as he sensed the custody officer had gone, he glanced round at the door, and sure enough the hole was now covered up. He was sitting on the edge of the narrow bed and he leant back against the wall, which was comfortingly cool. He began to relax. He was extremely tired now and his eyelids felt heavy. After a while, he closed his eyes.

He knows where the bastards are who car bombed the two off-duty soldiers in Londonderry. They've probably crossed south of the border by now. Fuck it. He'll go after them. Take the bastards on his own. For all he knows, he might already have crossed the border into the Republic. Which means the stakes have been raised and it's a highly dangerous game he's playing. Not just because he could end up in a ditch somewhere with a Provo bullet in the back of his head, but once he crosses over into the Republic, they know they have more to gain, more political mileage, by handing him over to the Garda. Then Dublin demands answers. What are British soldiers doing in the Republic of Ireland? And before you know it there's a political row between the British government and the opposition and the papers are screaming blue murder. Bang goes his army career. One of the elite. But that's assuming they take him alive. No fucking way.

He moves forward on his hands and knees, crawling through a ditch at the edge of a field. Everything looks normal. Ordinary countryside. But it feels hostile. He tries not to let that spook him. Keep calm; think clearly. Listen. Don't make any false moves.

He creeps slowly, covering hardly any ground. He has learnt to distinguish all the sounds he can ignore: the gentle rustle of foliage stirred by the breeze; the startled movements of rabbits and small animals. He stops to listen for a tell-tale human cough or muffled voice. Nothing. All clear. He crawls a little quicker now, across some rocks and into a small clump of trees. Just the other side of this copse, down a hill, is the derelict house. He watches the windows of the house, working out his best approach. Suddenly, a cough. Not a sheep nor any animal. A human cough. He peers through the foliage to his right, and less than a metre from his face, a man's legs; wearing khaki combat trousers. He lets his breath out slowly, wondering why the sentry hasn't heard him crawling through the copse. Then he hears a faint hissing noise, not unlike distant rain. What the hell is it? Through the fuzzy sound he can just make out a human voice, high pitched, excited. Then it falls into place. A personal stereo. It's Saturday afternoon. The sentry's listening to the racing on his personal stereo.

Slipping the long knife from his belt, he smiles grimly. It couldn't be easier. Do it quickly, before the race ends. If the poor bastard's horse romps home, he'll never collect. Ah well, the bookie always wins. He catches a glimpse of the man's startled face, sheer terror with the brief realisation that death is on him.

He slits his throat.

Evans opened his eyes suddenly. Disoriented, he sat up and looked around the small cell. He stared into space for a few minutes, trying to recall the recent events, as if this was something which had happened to someone else in a dream. He ran a hand through his hair, smoothing it down where it was sticking up at the back. Then he got up from the bed and began exercising, doing at least thirty press-ups to begin with.

Chapter 8

Major Denton stepped forward from behind his desk and offered Lambert his hand. 'Good to meet you, Inspector Lambert.'

It was a bone-crushing handshake. Lambert took it with as much sang-froid as he could muster, staring coolly at the SAS officer.

Major Denton gestured towards a chair. 'Take a pew. I'm not sure how much help I can be. However, I shall do my utmost.'

As Lambert sat, he realised he had to get a grip on himself. Things had not gone well on the journey from Swansea. He had been stuck in traffic because a lorry had jack-knifed in the centre lane on the M4, so that by the time he arrived at the SAS base in Hereford, he was in a terrible mood. Then he was kept waiting for half an hour before the major could see him. By now he was on a short fuse, and he hated Major Denton on sight. He hated the major's public school confidence and cut-glass accent, his conventional good looks and the self-satisfied smile simmering in his dark-brown eyes; and he despised the officer's careful grooming, the way his wavy, pepper-and-salt hair looked as if it was pampered each morning with a gentleman's hair lotion from somewhere suitably exclusive in London. Lambert realised his antipathy was irrational. He liked to think he treated everyone alike, whatever their race or background; but there was something about Major Denton that offended his sense of morality. Lambert felt he was in the company of cold-blooded, ambition. Here was a lawful killer who would one day, perhaps, become powerful enough to make life-and-death decisions from the comfortable distance of his Pall Mall club.

The major's head tilted back slightly before he spoke, fixing Lambert in his sights.

'Can I get you anything? Tea? Coffee?'

It was said without a trace of hospitality, making it seem like an imposition. Lambert toyed with the idea of inconveniencing him, then thought the better of it.

'No thanks.' Lambert glanced at his watch pointedly. 'I don't have a great deal of time.'

'Yes, well, I'm sorry to have kept you, but I had some pressing business. Matters of state security. I'm sure you understand.'

His expression deadpan, Lambert stared across the desk at the major and got straight to the point. 'Just before we apprehended Evans, you warned my sergeant that he could be dangerous. But he gave himself up without so much as a harsh word.'

Major Denton smiled confidently. 'One can't be too careful.'

'What sort of soldier was Evans?'

Without speaking, Denton turned towards the computer monitor on the side of his desk and tapped into the keyboard. Lambert knew he would have already gone through Evans's records with a fine toothcomb. So why this bullshit?

'Exemplary record, it seems,' said Denton. 'Distinguished himself in Northern Ireland.'

'Can you be more specific?'

Denton gave an apologetic shrug. 'Official secrets, Inspector. You'll just have to use your imagination.'

'I think I get the picture. He was one of your licensed killers.'

'He was a soldier, inspector. Highly disciplined, highly trained, fighting a dirty war.'

'One of Nietzsche's gentlemen?'

As soon as he'd said it, Lambert regretted it. Allowing his prejudices to show was not conducive to conducting a good investigation. But the major didn't seem put out by the remark. He shook his head with a weary smile.

'Evans killed a farmer,' said Lambert. 'A seemingly motiveless, pointless murder, with all the hallmarks of a professional assassination. Could Evans have gone over to the other side?'

Denton laughed contemptuously. 'Been turned around by the IRA? Inspector, we are in the middle of talks about decommissioning at this delicate time.'

'Look,' said Lambert impatiently, 'you and I both know there's the hardcore who don't want the talks to succeed. So could Evans have been working for them?'

Denton paused, regarding Lambert with disdain. 'It's possible. But unlikely. One thing's for certain. Evans never really belonged. Not to us. Not to anyone.'

'But he was a good soldier?'

'The best. Born to it.'

'What about family? Any military background?'

Denton went through the motions of glancing at the monitor. 'A maternal grandfather who served in the RAF. A reluctant conscript.'

'Did he have any friends in the SAS? Anyone he might have shared his secrets with?'

'He and a chap called Terry Clark were very close. They both left around the same time. Went freelance.'

Lambert frowned thoughtfully, wondering if this had anything to do with the murdered farmer.

'Mercenaries,' Denton explained patronisingly, thinking Lambert hadn't understood.

'D'you know where I can find this Terry Clark?'

Denton, knowing in advance that the inspector would ask for Clark's details, opened a desk drawer and handed him a sheet of A4 paper. The ex-trooper's address was handwritten across the centre of the page. Lambert looked deliberately surprised that the major had pre-empted his request for

Clark's whereabouts. If he already knew the information Lambert required, then why all the pretence of checking the computer for details? Perhaps it was simply because he enjoyed playing one-upmanship games, giving himself psychological advantages. Lambert could imagine him on the squash court, knowing all the little tricks that stopped just short of cheating.

'Lives in your neck of the woods, inspector.'

'Thank you.' Lambert glanced at the address, noticing that Terry Clark lived on the Mumbles, not far from his own place.

'But I don't think you'll find anything,' Denton pronounced, 'that connects the SAS with this killing.'

'Maybe . . .' Lambert began, then checked himself.

'I think not,' Major Denton said conclusively.

*   *   *

On the return journey, Lambert's mobile rang. It was Sergeant Ellis.

'Harry? It's Tony.'

Ellis always addressed him by his first name when they weren't in a formal situation. It was always 'sir' in front of other policemen, but there was a relaxation of the unwritten rules when no one else was around.

'Hi, Tony. What's the latest on Evans?'

'I've just come from the hospital. On Tuesday evening Evans was there, visiting his mother.'

'What's wrong with her?'

'She had cancer.'

'Had?'

'Yeah. Evans was with her when she died. Then, according to the nurse, he just legged it away from there as fast as his legs could carry him.'

'I wonder if her death's connected to the murder?'

'What's that?'

'Just thinking aloud.'

'How did it go in Hereford, Harry?'

'I met some stuck-up public school tosser who sounded as if he'd got a cork bunged up his arse.' He heard Ellis chortle at the other end of the line. 'I'm just on my way to see one of Evans's mates. Another trained killer. It shouldn't take long. I should be back around sixish. See you at our usual watering hole. Or are you feeling too knackered?'

'I think I could manage a couple of pints.'

'I'll see you later then.'

*   *   *

Terry Clark's house was tucked away in a side street on the Mumbles. It was a large fifties house, with new double glazed windows and a mock Georgian front door. Lambert compared it with his own one-bedroom flat, and took childish pleasure in the fact that at least the mercenary didn't have a sea view.

In the road immediately outside the house a stocky young man of around thirty was hosing down his gleaming electric blue Maverick four wheel drive. He had close-cropped hair, a pugilistic face – perhaps his nose had been broken in a fight – and a slightly weak chin. Lambert guessed that this must be Terry Clark. He parked the car further up the road, then walked back towards the mercenary's house. If Clark heard him approaching, he pretended not to notice.

'Did you know there's a water shortage?' Lambert announced.

Clark looked back over his shoulder, playing the insouciant hard man. 'So what? You from the council?'

Lambert passed his ID card in front of the mercenary.

'Are you having me on? This is Wales. We got plenty of water.'

Lambert smiled. 'Mr Clark?'

Terry Clark nodded uncertainly. 'You haven't come about the car washing, then?'

Lambert shook his head. 'Of course not. I'm afraid I've got some bad news. You probably heard on the news that a farmer was shot out near Pontardawe. I regret to inform you that your friend Gary Evans has been arrested and charged with his murder.'

The ex-SAS man's face was expressionless. For a while he stared at the stream of water running from the hose into the gutter. Lambert watched him closely, saying nothing.

'Mind if we go inside?' Clark eventually said, his voice slightly husky. 'I could murder a drink.'

Lambert followed him to the side of the house, where he turned the tap off, then in through the back door. The kitchen looked as if it had been recently refurbished, chosen from a standard design, and was rarely used for any serious culinary purpose. Apart from the remains of a Chinese takeaway, the surfaces were pristine.

The one reception room was spacious, the furniture smart, inexpensive and modern, predominantly black, with silver-framed posters on the wall, one of a heavy metal rock singer with satanic overtones, the other a black-and-white photograph of a nude on a beach, suggestively holding a beach umbrella between her legs.

Clark poured himself a liberal brandy and took a large gulp. It looked as if he was doing it for show. 'That's better,' he said, shaking himself like a wet dog as the brandy hit home. He held the bottle out towards Lambert. 'Inspector?'

Lambert declined and sat in an easy chair. Clark topped himself up, replaced the top back on the bottle and sat on the sofa opposite Lambert.

'Tell me about Gary's family,' Lambert said. 'It would be useful to know something about his background.'

'You know his mother just died.'

'Yes, my sergeant phoned me on my way over from – '

Lambert stopped himself from saying Hereford. 'Was he depressed about his mother dying?'

'Yeah. They were very close. I expect he took it bad.'

'When was the last time you saw Gary?'

Clark paused. He suspected the detective already knew the answer to this question. He took another sip of brandy before speaking.

'Day before yesterday.'

'That would have been Tuesday. What time Tuesday?'

Clark shrugged. 'Dunno. Could have been around two – half two. I'd just had me dinner and we met at a pub. Had some business to discuss.'

Lambert stared at the cocky, young mercenary, barely able to disguise his contempt. 'What about? War? Assassination? Arms dealing?'

Clark smiled arrogantly. 'It was all above board.'

'Was Gary planning to accompany you on your next – er – escapade?'

Clark shook his head. 'He knew his mother didn't have long to go. Said he was taking compassionate leave.'

'How did you know his mother died?'

'He told me, didn't he.'

Lambert tilted his head thoughtfully and stared at the heavy metal picture. 'I thought you last saw Gary Evans at lunchtime on Tuesday.' He shot Terry Clark a look. 'His mother died in the evening.'

Clark sighed impatiently and said slowly, 'I happened to phone him on his mobile. I wanted to talk to him about the little caper I had going.'

'What about Gary's father? Is he still alive?'

'He died about eighteen months ago. He was a roofer. One day he missed his footing and found out he weren't Superman.'

Clark's head lolled back and he snorted with laughter. Lambert stared at the mercenary, trying to place where he could have seen him before. Then an image of his father flashed inside his head, taunting him. The mercenary had the same laugh as his father and the same swaggering attitude. Lambert could visualise his father at this age, sporting a deadly charm that veered towards loathsome. He drove the memory of his father out of his head and threw his next question at Terry Clark.

'How did Gary take his father's death?'

'He was over the moon. Cracked open the champagne. And I don't mean your sparkling white. He hated his old man, he did.'

'Did he tell you much about their relationship?'

Clark showed Lambert a closed fist. 'Used to beat the fuck out of him. Thought he could teach him about God.'

As Clark stretched his arm out, the sleeve of his polo shirt rode up, revealing a discreet tattoo, but unmistakably the SAS insignia, the feathered dagger with its famous motto.

'Who Dares Wins, eh?' said Lambert, staring pointedly at it.

The young mercenary tugged at his sleeve, giving the impression that he regretted having had it inscribed on his arm. 'Who cares *who* wins?' he said.

'As long as you're not on the losing side,' Lambert offered.

Clark grinned confidently. 'My sentiments exactly.'

'Mr Clark, have you any idea why Gary Evans would want to shoot the farmer?'

'None at all.'

'He didn't ever mention it?'

Clark shook his head. 'Look, I ain't got a clue. I really haven't. Why don't you ask Gary?'

'We have.'

'And?'

'He's not saying.'

Clark grinned and relaxed back into the sofa. 'That sounds like Gary. Once he makes his mind up, that's it!'

*   *   *

The bar was quiet. It was a pub Lambert had discovered, quite a walk from HQ, and he and Ellis often came here to avoid other colleagues in the police service, who tended to drink in a public house nearer their work.

Lambert raised his glass. 'Cheers, Tony.'

Ellis looked at his boss, smiled and shook his head. 'You look like I feel, Harry.'

'Yes, well, it's all starting to catch up with me. The old man's funeral on Tuesday was not a good start to the week. And the bloody traffic today, that's done me in, that has.'

'You off home soon?'

Lambert nodded miserably. 'Such as it is.' The thoughts of an empty flat filled him with dread. He didn't relish a night of guilt and soul searching. He knew that if he spent the night indoors on his own, then his father's ghost, a contentious spirit in his memory, would provoke and torment him for hours on end.

'Well, I should try and get a good night's sleep,' said Ellis.

'Something tells me I'm in for a sleepless night, Tony. This murder's really playing on my mind. Normally, when I go home, I can usually manage to leave my work behind to a certain extent, but this . . . We've got a nice easy arrest, a confession, and enough circumstantial evidence to nail the bastard, but . . .' Lambert shook his head, sighed deeply and gulped back at least half of his pint.

'Yeah, I know what you mean. It's frustrating. Why would he shoot a useless old pisshead like that?'

'It doesn't make sense. He was obviously depressed about his mother, and he shot the old boy the following night. Coincidence?'

73

'What about the SAS and his time in Ulster?'

Lambert frowned thoughtfully. 'Yes, I can't help thinking it has something to do with the army. Or his mercenary activities.'

'Not that it makes any difference now. He isn' gonna say another word. I expect the defence'll go for a plea of insanity.'

'Well, I should think the CPS will agree to that. If he gets a life sentence in the funny farm, I don't think he'll see daylight again. I know one thing.'

'What's that?'

'I'd like that gorgeous, brown-eyed creature to help me unravel the sweeter mysteries of life.' Lambert inclined his head towards a far corner of the bar, where two girls had just sat down at a table.

Ellis gave his boss a knowing look. 'Complications. Who needs them?'

'Yes, you're right, Tony. Don't stray. It's not worth it. Now look at me: home to an empty shell and the sound of my own size nines. What I wouldn't give for a bit of female company just for tonight.'

Ellis grinned. 'Well, as it happens I do know someone who might oblige.'

'Oh, yes?'

'Yes. DC Maynard. She's really got the hots for you has Carol.'

Lambert thumped his empty glass onto the bar. 'No way, Tony. No way.'

Ellis looked at him quizzically.

'I've nothing against Carol personally. She's not bad looking. But I'm not going to risk making a fool of myself at work. I've mastered that in my private life.'

The barman, on hearing the slam of the empty glass, moved along the bar towards them.

'Another?' Lambert offered.

Ellis glanced at his watch. 'If it's all the same to you.'

'Yeah, go on home. You're lucky to be married to such a nice girl, Tony. Take a tip from me: don't screw it up.'

'I'll bear that in mind.' Ellis drained the last drop of his beer. 'So I suppose that's it about Evans, then.'

'Yes,' Lambert agreed with some reluctance. 'He'll go down for a very long time. And no one can force him to talk. End of story.'

Chapter 9

And that seemed to be that as far as the police were concerned. The motive for the killing preoccupied Lambert while he collected and prepared his evidence for the CPS; then he was told by the assistant chief constable not to waste any more time delving into the case. After all, they had as much evidence as they needed for a watertight conviction. But as the weeks went by, he forgot all about Evans. Other cases kept him busy, though most of them were straightforward, almost routine, compared to the Wilson murder: a man kicked to death outside a pub in Sketty; a petrol station robbery; an elderly woman brutally attacked in her home by a bogus water board official; and a spate of taxi driver robberies at knife-point. By the time the Evans case came to court, Lambert had made ten arrests and looked like getting as many convictions. But, if he had to admit it, as he sat in the courtroom listening to the evidence of this bizarre case, he underwent the same frustrated feelings of weeks ago. He wanted to know why. The Evans crime was more intriguing than any other case he had worked on; but this time it looked as if the motive for the murder was going to remain unsolved. 'Forget it,' the assistant chief constable told him, not knowing, or hardly caring, how deeply frustrating Lambert found it.

As for his private life in the weeks preceding Evans's trial, he realised he was now paying a heavy price for his infidelities. Home to an empty flat at night, which he tried to avoid by immersing himself in work. He had no hobbies, no interests outside of his job. He phoned Helen up a few times, under the pretext of talking to her about their daughter, but (perhaps because she was going ahead with divorce proceedings) she was always short, and her accusatory tone riled him. He visited Natasha several times, driving all the way to Leeds and stopping the night; but even his beloved daughter seemed irritated by her father's intrusion. She had new friends now, and her own life to lead outside the family home, which had ceased to exist. The times they spent together felt awkward for both of them, and Natasha felt sorry for her father and treated him with the long-suffering patience of a hospital visitor. On several occasions, he tried to chat up women in a Swansea pub, but they didn't want to know. Perhaps his charm carried the mark of desperation now. He began to take a long hard look at himself, what he had become. He was forty-six and, with his track record, should have made chief inspector by now, if not superintendent; but he suspected his superiors disapproved of his lifestyle and of the reasons for the break-up of his marriage. This could explain why his recent application for promotion had been denied, in spite of his excellent record as a detective.

As they waited outside the No. 1 courtroom of the Crown Court, Ellis said, 'Well, it didn't take long for the jury to decide. A result.'

Lost in his own thoughts, Lambert mumbled absently, 'It's not too late.'

'Something wrong, sir?'

'Just thinking.'

'I thought I could smell burning,' joked Ellis.

'It's never too late to change,' continued Lambert, turning towards Ellis and sharing his thoughts.

'No, I suppose not.'

'Have you taken Sharon out for a meal lately?'

Ellis frowned slightly, wondering where the conversation about his wife was leading. 'Well, we haven't had a chance to. Er, not lately. No.'

'You look after her. You're very lucky. She's a lovely girl.' Lambert's eyes blazed with conviction. 'Don't screw

77

up your relationship.' Then he smiled suddenly, realising he had perhaps shown too much vulnerability to a colleague. 'It's a case of do as I say, not as I do.'

Ellis tried to think of something to say, but his mind was a sudden blank. An image, not a pleasant one, popped into his head. Sharon alone with Lambert. It was highly unlikely this would ever happen, but just supposing it did. Would Lambert take advantage of the situation and attempt to seduce Sharon? Knowing his boss's bad reputation, could he really trust him alone with his wife?

'I would never try it on with the wife of anyone I knew,' said Lambert, looking closely at Ellis. 'That would be dishonourable. An abuse of friendship.'

Ellis was taken aback. It was as if Lambert could read his thoughts. He was embarrassed and mumbled, 'No, I never thought . . .'

He paused, struggling to finish the sentence. He was saved from the growing awkwardness by the sudden appearance of the court usher, swinging the courtroom doors open with a flourish, announcing the resumption of the trial. There was a flurry of activity, and a rush as everyone crowded into the courtroom for the sentencing. There were coughs and splutters, scraping and squeaking on polished wood as the court reassembled.

As they returned to their seats, the sergeant reflected on his boss's words. It seemed that Lambert had wanted Ellis to know, to reassure him, that their relationship went beyond the workplace and had grown into a deep friendship over the last few years. Ellis now felt a morsel of guilt hovering over his emotions like a hangover. He hadn't trusted Lambert. It seemed like a betrayal of their friendship. Brotherly love turned sour. On the other hand, Lambert did have a reputation . . .

Ellis was rescued from further squirming thoughts as the prisoner was escorted back to the dock. He and Lambert stared intently at Evans, watching for any hint of awareness in his eyes. But he stared unblinking into the distance. The judge returned, everyone rose in a perfunctory fashion, then sat again. The judge glanced at his notes briefly, and without once looking at the prisoner, addressed him through his lawyer.

'It is patently obvious that you have nothing to say. I think, therefore, that we must assume that you are unaware of what is going on. In view of the psychiatrist's report and your cursory confession, coupled with the circumstantial evidence, and the findings of the jury, I have no alternative but to sentence you to a term of life in a hospital for the criminally insane, where you will be looked after and where eventually some light may be shed on your motives for committing this terrible and futile crime.'

He gathered his papers together, rose and swept out, his manner suggesting that he was personally aggrieved by the prisoner's silence and wanted to wash his hands of the affair. As the rest of the court rose, Lambert muttered to Ellis,

'Short and sweet.'

As Evans turned away from the court, he caught Lambert's eye for an instant, and there was a glimmer of recognition. As soon as he had been taken down, Ellis turned to Lambert and said,

'Not a bloody word. Not since the day we arrested him.'

Lambert smiled cynically. 'A class act if ever I saw one. Come on, let's take a slow stroll back to the station.'

The walk back to the police station was hot and uncomfortable. Dark thunder clouds hovered and the inhabitants of Swansea grumbled and moaned, wishing the weather would make its mind up one way or the other. Hands deep in his pockets, tension in his shoulders, Lambert walked along the street with his eyes fixed on some distant time or place. Then, like a car braking, he suddenly stopped and turned to Ellis.

'Know what Evans reminded me of? That film of "Moby Dick". There was this South Sea islander who willed himself to die.'

'Queequeg,' offered Ellis.

Lambert frowned. 'Yeah, that's the fellow. How come you can remember his name? Film on recently, was it?'

Ellis grinned. 'I read the book.'

'Oh?' questioned Lambert, with what seemed to Ellis to be a touch of pique. 'I could never get past the first couple of chapters myself.'

Ellis shrugged apologetically. 'Well, you either love it or hate it.'

Lambert regarded his sergeant with narrow-eyed suspicion, as if his being able to read the book gave him some sort of advantage.

'I didn't love it or hate it. Just couldn't get through the bloody thing.'

Lambert turned and walked on quickly. They crossed Dilwyn Street into Singleton Street, Lambert broodingly quiet. He thought of Helen, the way she used to accuse him of only reading lightweight stuff. Which was true. He'd never been much of a reader.

They walked in silence for a while, Lambert lost in thoughts of his broken marriage, and Ellis not wishing to intrude on his boss's introspective mood. After a while, Lambert seemed to snap out of it, and returned to the discussion about Evans.

'D'you think Evans might be faking it?'

'Could be,' Ellis replied. 'I mean, he left the judge no choice but to commit him as insane.'

Lambert sighed with frustration. 'The whole thing stinks. He wanted everyone to believe it was a motiveless crime.'

'You think he might be covering for someone?'

'Who knows? But I do know one thing – and I'd stake my life on it – Evans definitely had a motive for murdering that farmer. The trouble is, now we'll never know. The motive's locked inside his head and I get the impression it'll stay locked up with him forever and ever. Amen.'

As he spoke, the still air was wrenched apart by a gigantic thunderclap. Then the heavens opened and people scurried for cover. By the time Lambert and Ellis arrived back at the station, they were soaked through.

Chapter 10

Lambert lay on his back, his arm getting numb under the gentle pressure of her neck, listening to the rain drumming on the roof. Her even breathing indicated that she had dropped off to sleep and he wondered if he could rescue his arm. He had enjoyed their lovemaking, but a doubt began to aggravate like toothache. He swallowed noisily as the post-coital calm shifted into reverse, and he was confronted by the spectre of remorse. He didn't want to hurt her; but it was inevitable that he would. Although he quite fancied her, they had little in common, and now it looked as if the entire Sunday was going to be spent in her company. Throughout the summer he had fought the temptation to ask her back to his flat, knowing it was a mistake, but things just got the better of him yesterday. Loneliness, that's what it was. Not to mention his physical appetites. Apart from one brief fling at the start of summer, with a married woman who ran for cover as soon as he suggested they see each other again, he had lived a life of celibacy for the last two months. But not from choice. He had tried ringing Melanie several times to ask her out, but she didn't want to know.

Apart from a recent freak heatwave, it had been a lousy summer, the wettest on record; but at least it seemed to keep the crime figures down. Although the chief constable was pleased with the seasonal drop in crime, Lambert had to admit that he was bored. He hated run-of-the-mill offences, however violent, and wanted to get his teeth into something more demanding. The last case that had presented him with anything resembling a challenge was the ex-SAS man who shot the farmer without rhyme or reason. And he'd been told to drop any further investigation into that one. Inexplicably, he looked towards the cordless phone on the bedside table, almost as if he expected someone to call. There was a slight pause, time playing tricks, and he guessed it would ring. When it did, it sent shivers of anticipation through his nervous system. The shrill bleep made his lover cry out as she was startled awake. He pulled his arm from under her, stretched across the bed, switched the bedside light on and picked up the cordless.

'I was fast asleep,' she said crossly.

'Yes, sir,' said Lambert into the phone. 'Yes, I was fast asleep.' He glanced towards his bedmate as she pulled herself into a sitting position, plumping the pillows behind her. With a smile, he ran a hand along her thigh and said, 'You disturbed a pleasant dream I was having, sir.'

His smile froze.

She was wide awake now. Something major had happened, she could tell. She felt Lambert's body tense with excitement, and saw the euphoric gleam come into his eyes.

'What? Of course I remember him. When? Right! I'm on my way.'

'What's happened?' she asked as Lambert moved quickly across the room, pulled open a chest of drawers and grabbed a pair of underpants.

'Remember that SAS man who killed the farmer? He's escaped.'

'You're joking!' she said, and swung her legs out from under the bedclothes.

'That's right,' said Lambert as he slipped his underpants on. 'I'm joking. That's why I'm going out in the middle of the night in this filthy weather.'

As she rummaged frantically under the duvet for her underclothes, Lambert watched her for a moment, admiring her slim body, then said, 'Get back to bed, Carol. It's just gone three.'

'You want me with you, don't you?'

He avoided looking at her while he pulled his trousers on. 'Not this time.'

'Why not?'

'I never mix business with pleasure. It's one of my rules. You'll be working on Keary's team from now on. Sorry.'

As he started to exit to the bathroom to splash cold water onto his face, she yelled out, 'Bastard!'

Lambert popped his head back round the door, smiling weakly. 'And you can see why, can't you, DC Maynard? That's no way to speak to a senior officer.'

He started to pull the door closed.

'Just a minute, Harry!'

'I haven't got a minute, Carol.'

'You owe me an explanation.'

She flushed angrily and thrashed around under the bedclothes until she found her bra and struggled into it.

'I've given you good appraisals, Carol. A great recommendation. And Keary needs a big team for that MP who was murdered. I said I could spare you.'

Her face was like a mask staring at him.

'So you already knew I'd be joining Keary.'

He gave her the hint of a shrug. 'We could never have slept together otherwise, Carol.'

He watched with astonishment as tears suddenly trickled down her cheeks like a tap had been turned on.

'I'm sorry, Carol. I really am.'

He closed the door gently.

*   *   *

'Come on, Tony. Come on,' Lambert urged as he waited for Ellis outside his flat. Raising the collar of his raincoat, he stepped out from under the porch and glanced up at his bedroom window. The light was still on, and he wondered what Carol would do now. Would she go back to bed and let herself out at a more respectable hour? Or would she storm off into the night and have nothing further to do with him? Somehow he suspected it would be the latter. How could he have been so dense? He had been convinced she'd be satisfied with the opportunity of working on a high-profile case. He had made the stupid assumption that she was a go-getter, looking for ways to climb the ladder to promotion. But underneath she was like so many of the women he'd hurt along the way: vulnerable and trusting. As the rain lashed his face, he indulged in remorse and guilt for a moment. Then he saw the flash of Tony Ellis's headlights and he brushed her out of his mind. He ran towards the car.

'Nice night for it,' said Ellis cheerfully as Lambert opened the door.

Lambert hesitated as he was about to climb in. 'Would you like me to drive, Tony?'

'I'll be all right.'

Lambert didn't push it. He knew Ellis had to prove to himself he was in control, in spite of the scars left by his parents' motor accident.

'You know where we're going?' Lambert asked as they took off.

'I had a quick look at the map. It's a place called Claywell, just the other side of the Brecon Beacons. Not that far from the English border.'

Lambert glanced at the dashboard clock. 'At this time of night, shouldn't take us more than an hour, I reckon.'

The rain lashed unrelentingly against the windscreen as they hurtled along the M4. They drove for miles without seeing any other vehicles on the motorway. Lambert experienced the weird sensation that they were drifting in water, lost in an uninhabited world. His imagination ran riot. He half expected to see a gang of Hell's Angels coming towards them through the night. Every so often, he thought he saw figures dashing across the motorway in front of the car. He rubbed the sleep from his eyes, and when he looked again at the road ahead, the figures had vanished.

Just before Newport, they came off the motorway and headed north. Because the road was flooded in places, the going became tougher, so that by the time they reached Claywell it had taken them almost an hour and a half.

Claywell was a small, nondescript town, and they drove down its main street and out the other side almost without noticing it. Ellis had been given directions from staff at the Claywell Hospital and easily found the light industrial estate about a quarter of a mile outside the town. He took the small turning opposite and drove carefully down a steep hill. At the bottom was an H roadsign, and round the next bend a high brick wall which they followed until they reached a heavy metal gate.

Ellis gave their names into the intercom and the gate swung open. 'Bloody hell!' he exclaimed as they drove into the hospital grounds. 'This is a *hospital*?'

'I think lunatic asylum is the proper name for it,' Lambert said with a grim laugh.

Ellis clicked his tongue disapprovingly. 'It's bloody disgraceful.'

'What is?' asked Lambert, though he could guess what Ellis was going to say.

'Treating people with mental health problems as if we lived in the dark ages.'

'Mental health problems is an understatement, Tony.'

'Even so,' continued Ellis indignantly. 'I mean, look at it. Talk about a building being typecast.'

The building, which had not been visible from the road because of the high brick wall surrounding it, seemed to grow out of the dark rocks of the surrounding hills. This was an early Victorian, Gothic monstrosity, as forbidding as it would have been almost two hundred years ago when it was a workhouse. Now it was lit by halogen security lights, giving it an even more eerie appearance, as if the building was being held under scrutiny by some invisible and malignant entity.

Two police cars were parked near the main entrance and Lambert saw a uniformed policeman on the front steps, talking to DC Wallace, who was inhaling deeply on a cigarette. Wallace gave them a cursory wave as they parked, then flicked his cigarette butt across the gravel drive in a shower of sparks.

As Lambert strode towards the building, Wallace rushed down several steps to meet him. He twitched his shoulders audaciously. Street credibility was part of his act. He was quite good looking in a chubby sort of way, giving the impression he had been pampered as a child, probably well into his teens. He sported a moustache, recently grown because of his baby-face looks. He greeted Lambert with, 'Lights out at ten o'clock, sir.'

'What the bloody hell you talking about, constable?'

Without waiting for a reply, Lambert barged through the front door. The sound of a forced laugh greeted him incongruously, as if he was a comedian making a stage entrance. That and an overpowering smell of bleach. He wheeled round on DC Wallace, waiting for an explanation.

'Ten o'clock. That's what time the inmates are bedded down for the night. So Evans could have had a four-or-five hour start.'

'And where's the idiot who's in charge of this open prison?'

Wallace tried to suppress a grin. 'Down the hall, sir. First on the left.'

*   *   *

Evans walked down the main street, keeping to the shadows of the shop doorways. His shoes squelched on the rain-soaked pavement and he stopped for a minute, thinking he

87

heard approaching footsteps. He slid into the doorway of a gift shop and waited, straining for the sound of feet on concrete. The only person who would be likely to be walking about a small Welsh town at four in the morning would be a policeman, so Evans braced himself for a confrontation. But, apart from the splash of rain and the distant gurgling of a river in full flood, the town slumbered comfortably. Even the houses seemed to snore. Perhaps the footsteps he could hear were the echoes of his own, or a trick of the mind. He sidled out of the doorway and continued walking stealthily along the street. This was a tourist spot, nestling in the mountains, so he guessed that there would be just the sort of shop he needed here. He found it, bang in the centre of the main street, next to a Copper Kettle tea room. The shop sold camping equipment, and here he would find everything he needed to survive. His hospital clothes were soaked and he looked forward to a change into dry clothing. Now all he needed to do was find his way round to the rear entrance of the shop and disable the alarm.

*   *   *

'Why did no one tell us?' Lambert demanded.

The hospital governor, clearly ill at ease, fiddled with a ballpoint pen, clicking it open and closed. He wore steel-rimmed glasses and his face reminded Ellis of Bill Sykes' dog. 'It didn't seem significant,' he replied, avoiding eye contact with the detectives.

'I don't believe I'm hearing this.' Lambert threw Ellis a look of stunned disbelief. 'Evans began talking again after he'd been here for only a month but you failed to inform us?'

The governor coughed nervously. 'Well, he'd been tried and sentenced. I – er – I thought he was going to be with us for a very long time, so there didn't seem much point in contacting the police.'

The governor gave Lambert a lop-sided smile, a point-scoring expression that was half apologetic.

'Well now,' Lambert said, squeezing the last drop of drama out of his delivery, 'he's been with you for only a short time. I appreciate the case was done and dusted, but we have no idea why he killed that farmer. And if Evans started speaking again . . .'

Lambert let the unfinished sentence hang like a portent over the governor and waited.

'He – er – refused to speak of his crime.'

'Refused, sir?'

'Well, yes. Any mention of his crime and he shut off completely. But in all other respects he became a model prisoner.'

'Didn't it ever occur to you that Evans deliberately chose not to speak? That he might have been planning something? The man is bright. You must have known that.'

The governor waved an uncoordinated hand about, searching for an excuse. 'Well, yes, but I don't see . . .'

Ellis, who was making notes, interrupted him. 'You say he became a model prisoner, sir. Was he allowed certain privileges?'

The governor hesitated slightly before replying. 'Well, he communicated with a librarian at the National Library of Wales in Aberystwyth.'

'Someone he knew?' Lambert asked.

'No, I don't think so. You see, Evans began to show a keen interest in Celtic mythology. We encourage our inmates to communicate with the outside world whenever possible. And this lady seemed to show a keen interest in Evans. They struck up quite a friendship.'

'Have you got copies of the letters she sent him?'

'Yes, but I don't think you'll find anything in them that

will shed any light on this. It was just an interest they both shared in all this New Age traveller stuff. Ley lines. Celtic stones and all that mumbo jumbo.'

'Ley lines?' Ellis said. 'Isn't that a sort of networking of ancient sites?'

The governor tugged his earlobe. 'If you believe that sort of thing. Personally, I don't. But it provided a focus for Evans. He practically papered his room with charts, maps of ancient sites and monuments that she sent him, and . . .' He broke off as the realisation caught up with him. His mouth opened, his eyes widened and the exclamation seemed to stick in the back of his throat. 'Oh, Christ Almighty!'

Now he knew it was going to be early retirement.

Lambert pounced. 'Exactly. You might as well have provided him with an Ordnance Survey map.'

*   *   *

During his time at Claywell Hospital, Evans managed to steal a pen torch and a cigarette lighter from the orderlies, which he concealed in the grounds. He also openly acquired some bulldog clips, saying he needed them to keep his Celtic notes in order. These, along with the appropriate tools, wire and a battery he had appropriated by breaking into a garden toolshed, would enable him to break into the shop. He managed to pick the lock without too much trouble. But he still had to smash the glass in the back door as there was a bolt holding it. Before entering, he paused for a moment to see if any lights came on in any nearby houses. But, apart from a row of cottages about a hundred yards away, most of the buildings nearby were mainly shops, and nobody seemed to have been disturbed by the noise. He pushed open the shop's door and slipped inside. Immediately the alarm began bleeping prior to going off – he probably had about thirty seconds. He ran his hand up and down the wall just on the inside of the door, found the light switch and risked switching it on. He was in a small room, used as a kitchen and partly for storage. The alarm setting was close to the back door, just above a draining board by a sink. He worked quickly to undo the screws on the box and this must have taken him about ten seconds – maybe more. Not much time left. Soon all hell would be let loose. Sweat began to run from under his arms and he tried to remain calm. He had less than ten seconds left. This was an alarm system with which he was familiar, but he needed to identify the sounder wire before he could cut it and attach it to the bulldog clip and battery. Using the cigarette lighter he burnt through one of the wires and, as luck would have it, the sounder wire was the first one he'd picked. Just as the alarm bell started its shrill jangling, he clipped on the bulldog clip wired from the battery and it was silenced. He'd made it. Breathing a sigh of relief, he wiped his sleeve across his forehead and mentally thanked Her Majesty's government for teaching him a few dirty tricks.

Another hour perhaps, and then milkmen, newsagents, and any other early morning risers would be starting to surface. He switched off the light, groped his way through to the shop and risked switching on the torch to find what he needed as quickly as possible. He found some military surplus clothes and a good pair of walking boots and quickly changed into them. He crammed a sleeping bag into a medium-sized backpack, along with a compass, a small cooking pot and a Swiss Army knife. And he couldn't believe his luck: in a drawer behind the counter he found a bar of chocolate. He stuffed it into the bag and began to pick up his discarded hospital clothes, intending to dispose of them in a dustbin along the way. But what was the point? As soon as they discovered the break-in, they would know who it was. Today was Sunday. With any luck it wouldn't be discovered until Monday morning, which would give him time to get well clear of the area. He dropped his old clothes onto the floor and began to fumble his way to the room at the rear of the shop. Some distance behind the shop, he remembered, was that row of cottages that looked like pensioners' houses, and he took the precaution of switching off the torch before going through to the back room, in case one of them got up to use the toilet and spotted the light. He crept forward, feeling his way in the dark, avoided knocking the tea and coffee mugs on the draining board by the sink, and was about to open the back door when he froze, his hand poised in the air as he reached for the handle. He thought he heard a human sound close by. A snuffling, padding noise, as if someone was creeping towards the back door. Someone who had seen the light from the torch and had decided to investigate? He had left the door slightly ajar and it seemed as if the person was starting to ease it open ever so slowly. His heart pounded against the wall of his chest. He took a deep breath and braced himself. He had no weapons he could use, other than the Swiss Army knife, and he cursed his stupidity for having put it inside the backpack. By now his eyes were used to the dark, and he saw the door open slowly another inch. This was someone trying to surprise him, he was sure of it. His right hand clenched into a fist, his body tense, but his mind high and clear from the rush of adrenalin, he flung open the door.

In the empty frame were the vague shadows of the black hills beyond the town. Nothing else. Then he looked down and saw a shadow dart across the yard, heard the scratch of claws and saw the bushy tail as it scrambled over the fence to safety. He grinned. An opportunist. Like himself. No, not like himself. He was no opportunist. It was all going according to plan.

*   *   *

As Ellis swung the car through the hospital gates, Lambert said, 'Hear the sound of drawers being opened and closed, Tony?'

'Sorry?'

Lambert chuckled. 'I think that's the hospital governor clearing his desk.'

'Yeah, I suppose the papers'll be screaming for his resignation. Everyone'll be after the poor bastard. He'll be the scapegoat.'

'Oh, don't waste any sympathy on that incompetent. He'll get what he deserves.'

'Yeah, but I can't help thinking it's the system. I mean, all he did was try to get through to one of the inmates. He's trying to understand them, improve their lives.'

'Hang on a second. We are not talking about mental health problems here. Not your old biddy who talks to herself and yells at passers-by in the precinct. We are talking mega dangerous, as in highly unstable criminals who have committed serious acts of violence.'

There was a pause as Ellis took a sharp bend with more acceleration than he intended and almost overshot the road into the opposite ditch. His tongue darted out and he wet his lips nervously. He remembered the piercing ring of the phone call at two in the morning, the herald of bad news. His mother had been killed outright, but his father had been cut by firemen from the bleeding wreck and died in the ambulance only a few minutes from the hospital.

Lambert, knowing that Ellis's parents' death still haunted him after all these years, made light of the situation. 'Careful,' he warned. 'Or I might have to go back and ask Wallace to drive.'

Ellis grinned in the dark. 'God forbid! Kevin thinks he's Steve McQueen.'

The car lurched, dipped and hit a great puddle.

'Bloody rain,' complained Lambert. He took a torch out

of the glove compartment, and shone it onto the bundle of maps and letters in his lap. He held one up, squinting as he tried to glean anything that made any sense.

'How d'you begin to decipher something like this?'

'Well, if Evans can do it . . .'

'Yes, but he knows where he's heading. And something tells me he's on a mission. This is all part of his plan.'

'Back to the SAS/IRA connection you reckon?'

'I don't know. None of it seems to make any sense.'

'How many miles d'you reckon he could cover in three or four hours, Harry?'

'Twenty, maybe thirty, if he's kept himself fit. If you were Evans, where would you go?'

There was a pause while Ellis thought about it. 'Well, I think I'd head for the city. It's much easier to get lost in a city. He might head for Birmingham or Wolverhampton. They're not that far away.'

'Hmm.'

'You don't sound convinced.'

'I don't know, Tony. I can't help feeling that Evans has got some unfinished business here in Wales. OK. It might be easier to track someone down in a rural environment, but in Evans's case . . .'

'Because he's trained in survival techniques?'

'Yes. And those blokes can live off anything that slithers, hops or crawls. And I have a very nasty suspicion he'll have a firearm stashed away somewhere.'

*   *   *

From his hiding place, Evans stared across the field towards the main road. He was tired, having covered over thirty miles since his escape, so it took a while to sink in. He knew he had the right location. He had memorised it perfectly from the map. There was the village just off the main road.

94

Not many houses, about sixty or seventy. A church, a pub and a small school, with a public footpath going from the church across the top of the field. It was definitely the right place. With one big difference. The oak tree and the lay-by had vanished. Now the area was being developed into a housing estate. Small starter homes, surrounded by scaffolding, the windows not yet in place, spread across the land at the bottom of the field, and bulldozers and JCBs lay idle in the swamp-like conditions after all the heavy rain.

Fuck his luck. So far everything had gone according to plan. Now he was without the Browning.

He heard a dog barking from the direction of the church. Judging by the light, he guessed it must be about seven-thirty or eight, and the village was beginning to stir. There was a wood about half a mile over the hill, and this was where he could spend the day. He was nocturnal from now on, and it was time he went to earth.

Chapter 11

The Sunday papers were already on the streets by the time the story of Evans's escape broke. But network television and radio used it as their headline news. BBC Wales, HTV and S4C put out special newsflashes, with a warning that Evans could be armed. During the trial, and because of the way Wilson had been relieving himself when he was shot, *The Sun* had dubbed Evans THE KARZY KILLER and the fact that Wilson had been urinating while he was shot was mentioned repeatedly, giving the bizarre impression that people were not safe in their own bathrooms.

Lambert was asked by the assistant chief constable to give a brief press interview, and he made his short statement around lunchtime on the steps outside police headquarters, assuring the public that Evans would soon be apprehended, but also warning anyone who spotted him not to approach him but to contact the police immediately. He gave short but courteous replies to their questions and adeptly avoided saying anything they didn't already know.

'How did it go?' Ellis asked him when he returned to the office.

Lambert shrugged. 'I used the sort of police jargon they expect to hear and, in short, told them nothing very much.'

'I hear Phillips is none too pleased that the full-scale manhunt hasn't begun yet.'

Lambert dropped his voice and leaned towards Ellis. 'Phillips is a dickhead. I'm glad the chief constable's got more sense than to listen to him. Evans is no fool. He'll have gone to earth. Our fox'll travel at night. Then we can let Phillips loose. Go boy!'

Ellis grinned. 'Come to think of it, he does look like a bloodhound.'

'Not *that* good looking.'

Lambert began flicking through his desk diary.

'A thought has occurred to me,' said Ellis. 'Could be Evans doesn't have a motive.'

Lambert looked up from the diary. 'Round the bloody twist, you mean? Yes, I'd thought of that. There's a full moon tonight. It looks as if Evans planned it this way. So if he is a sandwich short of a picnic, he's remembered to bring the bloody mustard.'

Ellis studied the ley line charts spread over Lambert's desk.

'What about these ley lines?'

'They look like copies of copies. And if he is travelling from one megalithic monument to another, surely he must have known that by leaving these behind in the hospital we'd have found them, then all we have to do is post police at all the ancient sites within a certain radius and wait for him to show up. But something tells me it's not going to be that simple. Still, I reckon she owes me.'

'Sorry?'

'Helen. My ex. She was into all this crap. Celtic wizardry.'

'I thought that was when they beat Rangers.'

'Ha-ha.' Emphasising the soft C, Lambert said, 'That's Celtic, dumb-brain.'

DC Wallace strolled nonchalantly into the office, hands in pockets, whistling lightly. His attitude immediately irritated Lambert.

'I thought you were looking into Wilson's background, constable.'

'I have. And I think I got a result.'

Ellis looked impressed. 'That was bloody quick.'

Lambert regarded him suspiciously. 'Come on then, constable. Enlighten us.'

'Well, Wilson came from Tregaron originally. He came from a pretty rough family by all accounts. Always in trouble with the police. But for minor misdemeanours. Poaching, petty theft, receiving, that sort of thing. His father died in a road accident forty years ago. Staggered out of a pub one night, got in his car and ran it into a tree. His mother had run off six months prior to this with another man. Never been seen since. Wilson had a brother, and he and his brother inherited the farm from their uncle. His brother kicked the bucket ten years after they took over the farm. Nothing suspicious. A heart attack. Apparently, there's no Irish connection anywhere.'

Wallace jerked the lapels on his grey leather jacket, preening himself.

Lambert congratulated him and asked how he had got the information so quickly. Wallace laughed and tapped the side of his nose.

'Come on, constable. I have to know.'

Wallace's moment of triumph seemed to ebb. 'Well, it was on the BBC news.'

'What? How come?'

'Apparently, they mentioned he was from Tregaron months back, after the shooting. I got in touch with the reporter and he filled me in on the details.'

'So it was a nice easy result, constable,' said Lambert. Rather grudgingly Ellis thought. Wallace's face was deadpan. It was hard to know what he was thinking.

'Still, it was a result, that's the main thing,' Lambert added.

Although Wallace's face remained expressionless, his eyes glowed briefly. Lambert was aware of the young detective's childlike need for compliments; the craving for appreciation. But there was something desperate about the way Wallace always tried a little too hard to please which made Lambert and his colleagues feel uncomfortable and just a little bit irritated. Avoiding the young detective's eyes, Lambert glanced down at the map on his desk and tapped his finger on the surface for emphasis.

'I'll see if Helen can shed any light on this. What I'd like both of you to do is to get me as much on Evans's mother as you can. Past history. Everything. A.S.A.P. Oh, and sergeant?'

'Yes, sir?'

'Drop these charts off at Helen's first, would you?'

Ellis looked uncomfortable. 'What about you, sir?'

'You mean, why don't I go round? No, I don't really want to see her. Things are . . . well, she likes you, Tony. Thinks the sun shines out of your arse.'

Lambert walked over to a map, covering a large area of south Wales. Pointing his finger at a spot on the map, he said, 'Here's the hospital. We have no idea which way he may be heading. For all we know, the ley lines could be leading us up a blind alley, something he's rigged up to mislead us. Now, supposing he escaped around one a.m. – we know it couldn't have been earlier because one of the orderlies did his rounds and swore blind he looked in on him – what would be his first port of call? Put yourself in his place.'

'Somewhere where he can get some warm clothes,' said Wallace.

'Yes, a clothing store,' agreed Ellis. 'And he knows it's a Sunday, so any break-in might not be discovered until Monday morning.'

Wallace clicked his fingers. 'But not necessarily an ordinary clothes shop. He's an SAS guy. He'd go for maybe an army surplus store.'

'Yes, or a camping shop,' said Lambert, staring at the map. 'That way he can kit himself out with everything he needs. So how much ground could he have covered last night? He's kept himself fit, we know. But it was raining and cloudy last night, so that would have slowed him down.'

'And,' Wallace added, 'it would depend on whether he went across country or used the roads.'

'He could jog much quicker along the road,' said Ellis.

Wallace gave him a condescending look. 'I think it's called yomping, my old mate.'

'Sorry?'

'That's what the SAS call it. Yomping.'

'Whatever,' Lambert cut in. 'We're probably looking at a radius of thirty miles, top whack. Get on to the local police and get them to check all camping stores for signs of a break-in. At least this way we might get some idea of where he's heading. Call me as soon as you get anything.'

Lambert picked his mobile up from the desk and started towards the door.

'You wouldn't be going to Aberystwyth, by any chance?'

'Got it in one. It's just possible that Evans might have an accomplice. I'm going to check out his pen pal from the National Library.'

Chapter 12

Gwyneth Chandler's detached cottage was high on the side of a hill, up a steep bank, on a narrow road a few miles outside Aberystwyth. Opening her front door to let her cat in, she saw Lambert's car pull up. Because she wasn't expecting anyone, she thought the visitor was calling on one of her nearest neighbours, someone who lived in one of the four terraced cottages about twenty yards from her own. She picked her tabby cat up and it immediately turned its purr on like a motor. She tickled it fondly under the chin, watching as Lambert got out of the car. Making a quick appraisal of the visitor, she put her lips close to her cat's ear and whispered,

'Not bad looking. I thought my luck had changed, Bran bach.'

The visitor looked up at her and began to climb the bank. 'Miss Chandler?' he called out.

She looked surprised and let the cat down. As Lambert approached, he noticed the surprise change into an expression of unease. He flipped his ID open in front of her.

'Miss Gwyneth Chandler? Detective Inspector Lambert.'

He saw fear in her eyes and heard the shallow intake of breath.

'Oh, God! What's happened?'

'It's about Gary Evans. Your pen pal from the asylum.'

Like air escaping from a balloon, she let her breath out slowly. 'God! That's a relief. I thought you might have been calling about my daughters. It's half-term and they flew to Canada last night to be with their father. They're a bit young really to be flying on their own, but . . .'

Lambert smiled apologetically. 'No, it's nothing to do

with your daughters. I'm sorry, Miss Chandler. I didn't mean to alarm you. I'm sorry.'

Gwyneth Chandler felt a sudden surge of anger. 'And it's *Mrs* Chandler, by the way.'

'I'm sorry,' he began, 'I thought . . .'

She caught him looking at the lack of a wedding ring on her finger.

'We separated,' she explained, testily. 'We never divorced.'

She stared back at him. There was a challenge in the look. A mixture of anger and sexual confrontation. Her eyes were cool green, diffused, the reflection of a forest in a lake. But also warm and teasing. She was, he guessed, in her mid-forties. Her attractive, auburn hair was soft and silky, gripped in Grecian style, upwards away from her face, although two wispy tendrils fell in front of her ears. She wore poster-red lipstick, which should have clashed with her hair but was somehow promisingly sexy on lips that were full and shaped into a letter M, as if she had sucked her thumb throughout her childhood.

'About Gary Evans,' he said.

'What's happened to him?'

'You haven't seen the news this morning?'

'No. Sometimes I listen to the radio. But not this morning.'

'I'm afraid Evans escaped in the early hours. He may be armed – and certainly dangerous.'

Her eyes widened with genuine surprise. 'Dangerous? In all his letters he sounded so . . . normal. Harmless.'

'How long had you known him?'

'Since we started corresponding. Some time in late August.'

'Not before?'

A lightning flash in her eyes. She knew she was under suspicion.

'No, of course not. I didn't know him from Adam.'

'What did he write to you about?'

'Celtic history. Myths. Legends.'

'Anything else?'

She shook her head.

'Did he tell you about his exploits in the SAS?'

'I didn't even know he was in the SAS. Although . . .' She hesitated.

'Yes?'

'It was just an impression I got. Most of the legendary figures he talked about seemed to be Celtic warriors.'

'Have you still got his letters? I'd like to see them.'

'Of course. They're inside. Would you like to come in?'

She stood aside, holding the door open, and he entered. Although he was only of average height, he still had to duck to get through the small doorway. As she started to close the door, the cat, which had been rubbing itself against her legs, darted outside. She tutted at its fickleness before shutting the door, then explained a touch apologetically,

'The hospital, when they asked me if I'd mind writing to him, told me he was a murderer. But that's all. They didn't tell me who he murdered.'

'It was without any apparent motive. A drunken old farmer. A nonentity. A nobody.'

Gwyneth Chandler frowned fiercely as if she was trying to remember something vital. Or perhaps she disapproved of the offhand way he had written off the victim of the crime. She moved across to a Welsh dresser, tugged open one of the drawers, and indicated an antique pine table in the centre of the room.

'Please sit down.'

As Lambert sat, he stared at the tight round curve of her bottom. She wore clinging faded blue denims with a pale green T-shirt tucked inside. She didn't look like a stereotypical librarian. There was something of the hippy about her, and he pictured her as she might have been in the late sixties, a swinging teenage flower child. And her figure was beautifully trim for someone in a sedentary job.

As she turned to hand him the letters, she caught him staring at her, felt his eyes undressing her, appraising her figure. She hesitated, clutching the ribbon-bound package in both hands, and smiled tantalisingly.

'You must have communicated regularly.' Lambert indicated with a nod the bundle of letters. 'That's quite a lot of letters for less than two months.'

'Only six or seven. About one a week on average.' She placed the bundle on the table in front of him. 'Excuse the mess. Would you like a tea or coffee?'

'Cup of tea would be welcome after that drive.'

'Sugar?'

'No thanks.'

She went out past the staircase, through a door leading to the kitchen. Before reading the letters, he looked round the room quickly. Two rooms had been knocked into one and a large beam ran across the centre of the low ceiling; attached to the beam were a corn dolly, several love spoons and some blue and white china plates. Above a polished slate fireplace hung a black-framed reproduction painting of an old lady inside a chapel, wearing a paisley-patterned shawl. Blu-tacked to the surrounding walls were pictures in gaudy colours, the school efforts of her daughters. The carpet was threadbare in places and there were ethnic rugs that looked as if they had been randomly laid but were probably concealing the most worn parts of the carpet. A Celtic cross stood on the dresser, next to a pottery vase of dried flowers. A tower of paperback books, stacked near the leg of an easy chair, gave the impression of someone who dips into books, reading little and often. Home-made jams, neatly labelled, stood in a row on the narrow windowsill, next to a thin, smoked-glass vase with a half-burnt incense stick leaning out of its neck. The room was vaguely bohemian, giving the impression that the untidiness was deliberate, to make it homely and informal.

'Where have you come from?' she called out.

'Swansea.'

He heard her filling the kettle as he started to undo the letters.

'Now I remember,' she said.

'Sorry?'

She lit the gas, then appeared in the kitchen doorway, leaning against the doorframe, a hand placed on her thigh, the fingers splayed.

'That farmer who was shot. About six months ago wasn't it?'

Finding her pose and body language distracting, he nodded seriously and looked her straight in the eye. 'Almost to the day. Why?'

'He came from Tregaron, didn't he?'

Something inside Lambert alerted him. He kept any expression out of his face and took his time as he asked her, 'He hadn't lived there for thirty odd years. How did you know he was from Tregaron?'

'It was on the news.'

'But why would you remember a detail like that after a gap of six months?'

She laughed and shook her head. 'Because at the time I remember thinking: I'll bet that farmer was paying the price for something he'd done in the past.'

'I don't follow you, Mrs Chandler.'

'You must have heard the legend of old Tregaron. The people were very wicked. It was the Sodom and Gomorrah of Wales. And the people were punished for it. Old Tregaron was destroyed by fire and flood. But some of the inhabitants survived. And now their descendants behave as their ancestors did.'

'Which would explain the high crime rate of the area.'

She beamed at him, pleased they were on the same wavelength. 'Exactly.'

'And,' added Lambert, 'the sheep shagging and incest.'

Her smile changed to a scowl. 'Look, I know you think I'm being stupid, but there could be something in it.'

'You mean the farmer deserved to die for something that happened long ago, and Evans was the unwitting instrument of execution.'

'Well,' she replied defensively, her hand moving to her hip. 'Why not?'

'Because there are no such things as dragons, that's why.' He smiled condescendingly. 'There never were. They look pretty on a flag, but they never existed.'

She glared at him with a mixture of irritation and frustration before disappearing to make the tea. Irrelevantly, he wondered why she wore the lipstick out here in the country, miles away from anywhere. He returned to the letters.

Dear Gwyneth

Thank you for writing to me and sending me details of our ancient culture. You can't think how much it means to me being stuck in here maybe for life. I have always been interested in myths and legends and I really appreciate you going to all this trouble for me.

I have always been fascinated by all these ancient sites and monuments and how they are linked as if by some magic force. I am talking of course about ley lines. Because ancient warriors were more sympathetic to the earth forces and had instinctive intelligence which modern human beings seem to have lost, their traditions live on. We were never conquered, not by the Romans, not by anyone. It just seems that way. We, the true believers in the earth forces, have kept the flame alive for thousands of years, since long before Christianity.

I would like to trace these magnetic forces and link up all the ancient sites. If you could send me any diagrams or maps of ley lines I would be very grateful and

Lambert stopped reading. The impression he got was that Evans seemed to be stringing her along with his interest in Celtic mysticism purely to obtain maps of ancient sites. Either that or he was barking mad. Or perhaps he was trying to show her that he was a little bit unhinged but harmless. The letter seemed to have been written with great effort, each character meticulously scribed as if by a child who has recently discovered the knack of joined-up writing. It was a schoolkid's effort, grammatically correct, but stilted and formal.

His mobile bleeped. Ellis.

'It's Tony,' he announced. 'They discovered a break-in at a camping shop twenty-six miles from the hospital.'

'Definitely him, was it?' Lambert asked.

'No doubt about it, sir. He left his hospital clothes lying in a heap on the floor.'

Lambert laughed. 'Cocky, arrogant bastard. Go on.'

'It looks like he may be heading west, further into Wales. And I've got some more news.' Ellis paused dramatically, enjoying himself. 'Are you ready for this? Gary Evans's mother came from a village just outside Tregaron. She was a pretty tasty young girl apparently, and was crowned Tregaron Carnival Queen one year. Not long after, she leaves the district for good. Never goes back.'

'Afraid she might be turned into a pillar of salt? You know, sergeant, as in the Old Testament. Sodom and Gomorrah.' Ellis hadn't questioned his statement about Lot's wife. It was said purely for Gwyneth Chandler's benefit, and directed towards the kitchen, where he knew she was listening. 'Go on,' he said after a brief pause.

'Well, not long after, she leaves Tregaron, moves to Swansea and meets Ben Evans. They marry within two

107

months. And that's about it. But the interesting bit is the fact that she was a beauty queen. Remember the coronet we found at Wilson's farm?'

'How could I forget it? It kept me awake for quite a few nights. OK, Tony. Well done. Go home and get some rest. Tonight we go hunting.'

As soon as he had hung up, Gwyneth Chandler entered with two mugs of tea, as if she had been listening behind the kitchen door, waiting for him to finish. He was lost in his own thoughts and barely noticed the steaming mug of tea she placed in front of him. Her own she put on the dresser, then stood leaning back, her elbows on the wooden top, and her hips thrust suggestively outwards. Without thinking, he found himself staring just below her waist, to the tight V of her crotch.

'See anything that interests you, inspector?'

He was thrown slightly. He knew she was talking about the letters but had she deliberately imbued it with a double meaning? He coughed lightly before speaking.

'You think he believed all this guff he wrote?'

'Why not?' She nodded towards the chapel painting of the old woman. 'See anything else in the painting? An intruder who shouldn't be there?'

'It's been pointed out to me before. The devil in the old woman's shawl.'

'The point is,' she insisted, 'did the artist deliberately put the devil in the shawl? And if he didn't, how did evil manage to creep into the depiction of a religious scene?'

'Or how the devil did he get there?' he quipped.

She scowled, her eyes glinting fiercely. He found himself thinking how attractive she was. Then her eyes softened and her face relaxed as she realised she was being serious and uptight.

'You must admit,' she said, 'that strange, irrational things can happen. Things which defy explanation.'

'I'm a detective. I deal in hard evidence. Not sword-and-sorcery myths. I'll leave that to the computer nerds.'

She laughed, showing him a row of perfectly straight white teeth. He felt the urge to hold and kiss her passionately.

'Virtual reality,' she said, jokingly.

'The bullet that ended Wilson's life was real enough.'

'I'm sorry. I didn't mean to be flippant.'

He smiled understandingly. Relieving the tension.

'D'you mind if I hang on to the letters for a while?'

'What if I said I did?'

'In that case, I'm afraid . . .'

'No, of course I don't mind. So long as you can let me have them back.'

He rose and began to gather the letters together. 'Yes, I'll make sure you get them back.' Smiling at her. 'If I have to bring them myself.'

She returned his smile. 'That's what I meant,' she said.

He held her look for a moment, and felt as if there was a taut wire running between them, live and vibrant, pulling them together. He broke the spell by glancing at his watch and muttering, 'I have to get back.'

Although he tended to believe her when she said she hadn't known Evans until he corresponded with her after he'd been banged up, he still couldn't completely rule her out as his co-conspirator. And allowing his feelings towards her show in such an obvious way was nothing short of collusion with a suspect.

He let himself out, and when he glanced back at her, he caught the amused, knowing expression on her face.

'Drive carefully,' she said.

He risked another look deep into her eyes, one of those sexually promising exchanges. After all, he convinced himself, it was highly unlikely she was Evans's accomplice. And if ever there was promiscuity in an expression, this was as close as it could come.

'Be seeing you,' he said, as he walked down the slope to the car.

'Yes, don't forget the letters.'

As he drove off, he gave her a wave. She was standing at the cottage door holding her cat, which had appeared from nowhere and was now enfolded in her arms, being lovingly fondled and stroked. Lambert thought about the sensuality of her touch. And he thought about the looks that had passed between them and wondered if she was like a Siren, luring passing detectives onto the rocks like a gullible sailor. After all, she was a Lone Danger; a single parent on the lookout for a bloke. Perhaps searching for a relationship. Like himself. Or perhaps she was just looking for an adventure. Also like himself.

He looked in his rear view mirror. She was still standing at the cottage door watching as he drove over the brow of the hill.

Chapter 13

When he arrived back at his office, Lambert found Ellis and DC Wallace leaning over his desk, studying pages of ley lines.

'Any luck?'

Ellis demonstrated the futility of their search by puffing out his cheeks and blowing.

'No, sir. Without knowing his intentions, it's bloody impossible. Your wife's outlined in red some of the possibilities, but there are dozens of ancient sites at all points of the compass.'

'Wales is a mysterious country,' said Wallace.

Lambert glared at him. 'Don't you start. I've had dungeons and dragons up to here.' He turned to Ellis. 'So she wasn't much help then.'

Ellis felt awkward. 'Well, you have to admit, sir, if we can't work it out, why should we expect . . .'

Lambert interrupted him. 'Then why the bloody hell has she outlined some of the lines in red?'

'Because I told her of the possibility that he might have concealed a gun somewhere following the murder. She's just guessing, but there seems to be a pattern from the asylum to where the shop was broken into, then south-west across the Beacons to Pontardawe – the spot where he shot the farmer. If he did conceal a weapon, it can't have been that far from Swansea. Somewhere in this region, say. Now have a look at this pattern of ley lines.'

His eyes glued to one of the pages on the desk, Lambert said, 'He could either be heading north along this track . . .'

'But it doesn't seem to go anywhere,' said Wallace.

'Do any of them? Other than to a load of ancient stones.'

'No,' persisted Wallace. 'I mean, there don't seem to be so many sites north of Tregaron, up here in the Aberystwyth region.'

'I wondered why I hadn't spotted any cromlechs or burial chambers,' Lambert said, deadpan.

Wallace smiled dutifully.

'Shit!' exclaimed Ellis. He rushed over to the wall map, tapped his finger on a spot on the west coast and said, 'This is the last ancient site on this particular line.'

It took a moment for it to register with Lambert. 'That site's near Fishguard.'

'Probably overlooks the fucking harbour,' said Wallace.

'You said it, constable. Harbour. The Irish ferry. I still haven't ruled out an Irish connection in all this. It could be a complete waste of time, but you never know.' He grabbed the phone and started dialling. 'I'll get onto Phillips.' While he waited for an answer, he said to Ellis, 'Incidentally, sergeant: she's not my wife anymore. Decree absolute came through last week.'

Ellis was uncertain how to respond to this.

'Oh. Er – congratulations?' he said.

*　　　　　*　　　　　*

The house was on the market, several prospective buyers had shown an interest, and still Helen hadn't made any progress in finding another property. She sat on the sofa in the living room, the coffee table piled high with papers and leaflets. She found it difficult to concentrate. Her attention was divided between deciphering estate agents' euphemisms and mind-numbing arguments about the Euro on the television news.

She sighed discontentedly and absently picked up a photocopy of the map of Welsh ley lines Tony Ellis had left her. There was something nagging away at the back of her mind, something to do with the map. But she couldn't work it out. Every time she returned to it, she stared at it helplessly, and felt something tugging, pulling her towards something that was just out of reach. It started to get on her nerves. Half of her wanted to help with the police investigation, then she wondered why on earth she should put herself out for her husband. Especially as he was now her *ex* husband. Signed, sealed and settled. Let him sort out his own investigation. Let him overlook vital evidence and take the consequences. Serve him right for being such a narrow-minded pragmatist with no interest in his own culture, denying his atavistic sense of being and deep-rooted traditions.

Annoyed with herself for becoming so involved with *his* problems, she slammed the photocopy on top of the estate agents' details and was relieved by the distraction of a change of news item on television. Shots of police. Dog handlers with obedient German shepherds at their side. The camera panned over the darkening hills and came to rest on a male reporter, windswept and wearing a safari jacket better suited to an assignment in a war-torn desert than the cold, sun-shrinking autumn in the Welsh mountains. He stood slightly hunched to emphasise how cold he felt, and stressed almost every word in his delivery.

'And as the large-scale manhunt gets under way to track down Gary Evans, the ex-SAS mercenary and killer, who last night escaped from Claywell Hospital for the criminally insane, an investigation is being carried out concerning the security of this and other such hospitals. Meanwhile, the killer remains at large, and a police spokesman has indicated that it seems likely, due to Evans's army training, that he may wait for the cover of darkness before he makes his move. But just where he is heading is anybody's guess. This is Vernon Collins for BBC Wales.'

The camera panned away from the reporter and picked up a helicopter as it soared dramatically upwards, bang on cue, as if these events had been contrived. Then the picture cut back to the studio. The newsreader turned over a page and began reading from the autocue a story about sextuplets born to a woman in Edinburgh.

Helen picked up the remote and switched the TV off. That same unsettled feeling nagged at her. She found it difficult to concentrate on anything for very long. She began to dwell on the past, remembering the good times. And, inevitably, her thoughts turned slowly to the what-might-have-been of their lives in the future. If only he could have been more like his sergeant. Tony Ellis seemed the loyal type. A bit dull, perhaps. But loyal. And, given the benefit of hindsight, she would gladly have traded charismatic charm and compulsive infidelity for good honest solid dullness.

*   *   *

With Wallace driving, the car hurtled round a bend on the outskirts of Swansea. Ellis was sitting next to him, and Lambert could see the muscles in the back of his neck, wire-taut with tension. He knew what Ellis was going through, the silent suffering.

'OK, Kevin,' said Lambert as he pulled himself upright in the back seat. 'I'm impressed. You've proved you can drive Hollywood style. Now for Christ's sake slow down long enough for me to dial my mobile.'

'Sorry, sir,' said Wallace, easing his foot off the throttle.

Ellis stared silently ahead at his vaguely disconcerting reflection in the windscreen. He was aware Lambert had cautioned Wallace for his benefit, and he felt exposed. He wanted to conquer this gut-wrenching fear of speed once and for all. Although he was grateful whenever Lambert came to his rescue, and appreciated the understanding nature of his boss, there was another part of him that found the intervention irritating.

114

Lambert's voice boomed from the back as he spoke into his mobile. 'I want a watch put on the port at Fishguard. Hello? Did you get that? Shit. I'm breaking up. Fishguard. The port at Fishguard. We think that's where he may be heading. No! Not tomorrow. Now! I know he's on foot, but he could always hot-wire a car. Did that thought never occur to you? Yeah. And the same to you.' Lambert switched his mobile off. His voice dropped to a calm, dismissive level. 'Bloody moron.'

Grinning, Ellis exchanged a look with Wallace. As the car joined the M4, heading towards Carmarthen, Lambert peered out of the window.

'Look at that,' he said. 'It's cleared up. Full moon and not a cloud in the sky.'

Ellis chuckled. 'That's what you call perfect planning.'

'He couldn't have planned the bloody weather. He's just one hell of a lucky bastard.'

           *   *   *

Smelling of damp clay, and pushing to one side the bracken and wood he had used to conceal himself, Evans crawled out from his hiding place. Having been confined in a cramped space for over twelve hours, his muscles ached and it took him a while to adjust to the freedom of being able to stand and move around. He was desperately thirsty and needed to find a mountain stream. But first he needed to lay a false trail. Nothing too obvious.

He looked up at the sky, seeing a moon so big it looked as if it might collide with the earth. And thousands of stars, cold and bright, reminding him of the night he and his mother had stayed late at Porthcawl, shivering in a shelter on the sea front, gazing at the mystery of the clear night sky, trying to identify the constellations, although neither of them knew enough to tell the Bull from the Great Bear. He stared up now with the same sense of wonder he had felt as a child.

A dog barked in the distance, reminding him that the police were getting close. He ran swiftly across the moonlit field, his legs brushing the long grass with a rhythmical swishing sound. At the end of the field was a gate with a strip of barbed wire entwined along the top bar. He climbed over it carefully, then turned and deliberately snagged his sleeve on the barbed wire, checking to see if any fibres remained attached to the barb. Just to make certain, he felt inside his jacket and tore one of the buttons off his shirt, letting it drop to the ground by the gate. Then he continued running, crossing the field, treading heavily in the mud where the meadow dipped in the middle. If they came this way, they would be almost certain to see his footprints going straight across, leading them south-west along this ley line to an Iron Age fort about two miles away.

When he reached a stile on the other side of the field, he took the chocolate wrapper he had saved from his pocket, screwed it into a ball and let it drop to the ground. Another bark, closer this time. He had to hurry. He undressed quickly, taking off all his clothes, including his underwear, and stuffed them into his backpack. Then, carrying his boots, he ran around the northern edge of the field back towards the gate. He avoided crossing it and scrambled over the dry-stone wall instead. He could hear them now, getting closer, probably entering the wood on the other side, less than a quarter of a mile away. That morning, as he dug himself an earth in which to hide, he had noticed cows grazing in the field near the trees. Now, as he ran towards the wood, he searched desperately for the dark patches of their droppings. As soon as he found one, he crushed it with his foot, breaking the crisp exterior, squelching the liquid manure inside. He knelt down, scooped handfuls of it, and rubbed it all over his body. A survival trick he'd learnt for outfoxing tracker dogs, but had yet to put to the test.

He thought he could detect voices now. Shouts. He hadn't

116

much time. He raced for the trees and the path that led through the middle of the wood. He ignored the stinging pain in the soles of his feet as he charged barefoot into the blackness of the wood, barging into trees and crashing through the dense thickness of shrubs and bushes. He realised the noise he was making would soon be picked up by the dogs so he stopped beneath a large oak, tied his boots together and slung them around his neck on top of the backpack. He took a deep breath then leapt for the nearest branch and pulled himself up, clambering quickly through the leafy thickness. Because it was so dark, he shut his eyes against the branches that pricked and scratched, climbing blind. Then he froze as he heard voices close by, and he prayed that the noise of his assent had gone undetected.

'Just think of the overtime, John.'

'Yeah. It'll all go to the bloody tax man.'

The voices came from immediately below him, and judging from their conversation he was in the clear. Suddenly, the beams from their torches shone upwards all around him, dancing off the leaves. He tucked himself into a tight ball, hoping that his bulk was hidden by the thick lower branches of the oak. His breathing was loud and tremulous and he was scared the dogs might hear him. The dog handlers were just below his tree now. He could hear the dogs panting and sniffing. His hands gripped the branch tightly, his body embracing it, naked and vulnerable, but at the same time exhilarated by his instinct for survival.

A sudden thunderous roar startled him and he almost lost his grip on the branch. For some strange reason he hadn't heard the chopper approach. It hovered over the tree like a stuttering monster and the draught from the blade stirred the leaves. He thought the game must be up now. Their forward-looking infra red would pick up the heat from his body and it would soon be over. There was no way out. He was trapped. He looked up and through the branches he saw the

117

dark underbelly of the chopper, its great beam arcing over the countryside like a giant eye.

He waited, knowing that contact would be made with the police below and in just a few moments he would be back in custody. But in an instant the chopper tilted sharply and zoomed away towards the meadow. And below him the sounds began to fade into the distance.

He waited, wondering why the thermal imaging had missed him. Then it came back to him, another of his lessons in survival. He'd been saved by the leaves of the oak. The last couple of weeks, just before the heavy rain came, the country had been sweltering in an Indian summer, so that the leaves had soaked up and retained the heat of the sun, which was all that the infra red imaging could pick up. And any images picked up from between the trees would be rightly taken as those of the search party.

He waited until he heard shouts coming from the distant fields before climbing down from his hiding place. He patted the trunk of the oak before moving off in the opposite direction to his searchers.

*   *   *

On the outskirts of Carmarthen, Lambert sighed long-sufferingly. 'I shouldn't have drunk all that coffee.'

'Yeah, I wanna go an' all,' said Wallace.

'What about you, sergeant?' Lambert asked.

'Well, I'm not exactly bursting but . . .'

Lambert interrupted him. 'Fair enough.' He tapped Wallace on the shoulder. 'Head for Carmarthen and stop at the nearest pub. We could all do with a short break.'

It was an excuse to stop and have a pint and they all knew it. But there was a tacit understanding that no one would mention it.

The first pub they found had one small bar. It was like walking into someone's front room. The few Sunday night regulars stopped talking when the three of them entered and mumbled a curious good evening. As soon as Lambert had bought three pints, his mobile rang. The regulars fell silent as he took it out of his pocket and stared at him with bovine interest. Wallace grinned, exchanged a look with Ellis, and whispered in his ear, 'This'll give the natives something to gossip about after we've gone.'

But Lambert exited hurriedly to take the call outside, clearly leaving the natives disappointed. Ellis carried Lambert's pint, and he and Wallace squeezed into a quiet corner in the L-shaped bar, away from the other drinkers.

Outside, Lambert pressed the mobile close to his ear. The line crackled and a voice surfaced like a gush of air.

'Inspector Lambert? Hello? Inspector Lambert?'

'Who wants him?'

'Sergeant Thomas here.'

A pause.

'Well, go ahead, sergeant. This is Harry Lambert.'

'We've found some fabric snagged on some barbed wire on top of a gate. And his footprints leading across a field. We also found a chocolate wrapper near the fence on the other side. Looks as if you were right, sir. He seems to be heading south-west.'

'Hmm,' Lambert mumbled doubtfully after a pause.

'Hello? You still there. Sir?'

'Yes, I'm still here. What are the chances, sergeant, of him crossing your line and heading back east or north?'

He heard the sergeant guffaw. 'No way. We've got dogs, helicopter, and we've called in . . .'

'Yes, yes, I know,' Lambert broke in impatiently. 'But this is Superman in khaki. I just want to know if there's the slightest possibility . . .'

'With all due respect, sir, I hope you're right about these lines thingummies. ''Cos if he don't follow them then we're wasting our bloody time.'

'How can I predict what he'll do?' Lambert snapped. 'I'm not telepathic.'

It was on the tip of the sergeant's tongue to say, 'No, but you're the bloody detective.' Instead, he reiterated forcefully, 'There's no way he can get through our lines. No way. Course, he could always nick a car and be anywhere in Britain by now.'

'But going by your findings, sergeant, you might not be far behind him by now.'

'Well, the chopper'll soon spot him then. But I'll tell you one thing . . .'

There was a loud gushing noise then the line went dead. 'Bloody mobiles,' said Lambert and returned to the pub. He joined Ellis and Wallace at their tucked-away corner of the bar and they sat huddled over the table, voices lowered. Lambert told them about the sergeant's evidence. Ellis was dubious.

'Sorry, sir, I know Sergeant Thomas is confident he couldn't head north and evade his men, but it's not impossible. Highly unlikely but not impossible.'

'What makes you say that?'

Ellis glanced at Wallace before speaking. 'Well, sir, Kevin was telling me about the methods of the SAS. Tricks to stay alive. Avoiding the enemy and all that. He's got stacks of survival and combat magazines at home.'

Wallace looked embarrassed. He mumbled, 'It's only an interest, like.'

Lambert grinned. 'I've got serious doubts about you, Kevin. You'll be telling me you collect Nazi war memorabilia next.'

Chapter 14

Going directly north, Evans walked four miles before he found a mountain stream, where he immersed himself in the freezing water and washed away the nauseating smell of cow manure. Then, having quenched his thirst, he dressed hurriedly and continued his trek north at a steady pace. His feet, lacerated by thorns and brambles, rubbed painfully against the new leather of the boots. He walked another six miles before he decided to rest. He was exhausted and hungry. He was tempted to look for a farm to steal some poultry but thought better of it. He didn't want to risk alerting a vigilant farm dog. He would have to hunt for his food the hard way. Then he remembered his opportunist intruder at the camping shop. The fox had chosen an easier lifestyle, living off human waste. It gave him an idea.

He knew from memory that he was close to an A road, and guessed that by now it must be nearly midnight, so he could easily risk walking several miles along the road, and if he heard a car approaching, or saw distant headlights, he'd have time to hide. Spurred on by the thought of food, he walked at a brisker pace now. The night was still. He could smell the clean crisp frost in the air, and heard the gurgling of a fast-flowing stream, falling and splashing over rocks. The effort of walking so quickly made him sweat and his back soon became soaked in perspiration. After walking for another twenty minutes, he came to a car park with picnic benches and litter bins. He thought of rummaging among the bins for scraps of food, then changed his mind. It was doubtful if anyone had picnicked here for months, so any left-over food would be rotten. At the end of the car park he crossed a cattle grid onto the main road and listened carefully for approaching cars but, apart from the sound of running water, it was quiet. He kept his eyes on the road and had gone no more than half a mile when he found what he was looking for: a rabbit, its head squashed by the wheels of a vehicle, but most of the body still intact. He peeled the carcass off the road and headed back onto the mountain, moving parallel with the road. He continued walking until he came to a dense forest of conifers. Skirting the perimeter, he came to a gate and a track leading into the interior. He climbed over it and walked along the path into the pitch black of the forest, knowing that if he lit a fire it would be obscured by the density of the trees.

*   *   *

Following the news of Evans's escape, inevitably the police received dozens of calls claiming he'd been seen. The most recent report came from a British Telecom engineer who spotted a youngish man with short hair getting into the back of a BMW parked in a deserted beauty spot in the Mynydd Preseli National Park, not far from Fishguard. But when the three detectives got there, hoping to surprise their man as he snatched some sleep before catching the early morning ferry for Rosslare, it turned out to be a false alarm. Having crept slowly across the picnic area, they threw open the rear doors of the BMW to find a man with red hair, and not particularly young, lying on top of a woman who screamed loudly. Ellis flipped open his ID, while Lambert mumbled an apology and slammed the door shut. Wallace, at the door on the opposite side, stared at the lovers a bit longer, grinned and said, 'Carry on, sir.'

This had been around four a.m. Following this incident, Lambert told Wallace to drive to the next picnic area and to pull in and wait. The car heater was turned up to high with the engine idling. Lambert stretched himself out on the back seat and muttered sleepily,

'Waste of bloody time.'

'At least it gave Kevin a chance to exercise his driving skills,' said Ellis jokingly, though there was a slight tremor in his voice as he recalled the recent hair-raising race to catch their potential quarry.

After a while all three of them fell into a light sleep. Wallace stirred after ten minutes and switched the engine off. As Lambert dozed, he had one of those dreams where he knew he was dreaming, and surrendered to the surreal images which bombarded him. A woman hanging from Stonehenge; a jellyfish floating near the seashore; his father kissing him with beery breath; a girl on a cloud, dressed like a Judy Garland in *The Wizard of Oz*, waving at him as she floated away; his mother lying in hospital having a blood transfusion; maps of Wales, with fiery dragons burning through the parchment.

Wallace coughed and Lambert started. He woke, and spent some time thinking about his relationship with Helen. He realised he had behaved exactly like his own father had towards his mother. No, not exactly. His father hadn't spared his mother's feelings, hadn't even tried to hide the fact that he screwed around. His father had been a misogynist, and he had been an only child who was devoted to his mother, and perhaps that was the reason why he loved women so much. He wanted to love them all, to make up for his father's shortcomings. Or was that just an excuse? And did the reasons matter if the end result was the same? Helen had been hurt, just like his mother. History repeating itself. The arguments went round and round in his head until they gradually disappeared, tapering into a long black tunnel of sleep.

He woke again, this time with an icy stab of pain slicing into his face. His cheek was pressed against the cold of the window. He shivered, yawned loudly and rubbed the sleep from his eyelids.

Ellis, sounding as if he'd been awake for some time, said, 'I feel like an old dishcloth that's been used to clean out the bog.'

'That good, eh?'

Wallace, awakened by their voices, jerked his head into an upright position. 'Christ! What time is it?' he said.

'Dawn,' Ellis replied. 'Look at that.'

The sun came up over the craggy, purple mountains like a golden apple, juxtaposed to the rice-paper moon which was slowly fading, and the sky was streaked with delicate brushstrokes of pink.

'Just going to stretch my legs,' said Lambert.

Ellis swung open the car door. 'I think I'll join you.'

Wallace turned the ignition on and complained about the cold.

Lambert walked to the edge of the picnic area, and stood at the top of a hill, gazing at the breathtaking sunrise. Ellis arrived quietly at his side.

'Makes you feel almost religious,' he said.

Lambert was non-committal. 'I suppose.'

'You know, once Evans broke into that shop, and we had an idea which way he was heading, I thought we had him. I thought there's just no way he can avoid being seen by someone. You think we've lost him? I mean, really lost him?'

Lambert shrugged. 'It's a test. Like he's deliberately pitting his wits against ours. And so far he's ahead of the game. He's winning. We've done everything he wanted us to do from day one. From the moment we found the body. It's a trail. He's leading and we're following.'

'But where?'

'If we knew that . . .' Lambert shivered and turned the collar of his jacket up. 'I feel like we're acting out some sort of scenario for Evans's benefit.'

'I know what you mean. We have to guess his next move.'

Lambert turned to face Ellis. 'No, what we have to do is find the motive for his crime. Christ. I'm losing my grip, Tony. Ever since Helen and I split up, I've been . . . floundering. I've overlooked so many obvious things.'

'For instance?'

'I ought to hand in my notice right now. Right. Let's get back to Swansea.'

Lambert turned and walked purposefully towards the car. Wallace was leaning on the bonnet, deeply inhaling on a cigarette.

'It's a bit drastic, isn't it?' said Ellis, hurrying to catch up with his boss.

Lambert stopped. Puzzled. 'What is?'

'Giving in your notice.'

It was said with a poker face and he wondered if Ellis was joking or not. Then he caught the twinkle in his sergeant's eye. He ignored it and began counting off points on his fingers.

'Right. I want to know the blood groups of Evans's mother, his father and Ted Wilson. Check their hospital records or their doctors. And check Evans's bank transactions prior to his arrest. He only had a balance of six hundred quid in his account. Not much for a soldier of fortune.'

His hand on the car door, Lambert turned and glanced towards the spectacular sunrise. 'I think there are ghosts in the machine,' he said.

'I'm sorry,' said Ellis. 'You've lost me.'

Lambert, after savouring a dramatic pause, explained, 'It's a distinction between the material body and the immaterial soul. Evans is one hell of a fighting machine. And I just wonder what ghosts are controlling him.'

*　　　*　　　*

After his meal, cooked over a small fire of pine cones, Evans felt a new surge of energy and managed another twelve miles before it began to get light. Arriving close to a village east of Lampeter, he concealed himself in a small thicket surrounded by a barbed wire fence and prepared himself for the long and tedious wait for nightfall again, lying curled up in a ball, his knees against his chest. Within minutes he drifted into a deep dreamless sleep.

Hours later, he was woken by the sound of children's voices close by. Just the other side of the fence was a large oak tree overlooking a muddy hollow that looked as if it might once have been a pond. There were two of them, boys of about twelve or thirteen, standing on the ridge overlooking the hollow. One of them had a gun and fired at his friend. Instinctively, Evans counted the rounds. Eight caps cracked in rapid succession. The boy without the gun, clutched his stomach and dived out of sight into the hollow. The one with the gun continued clicking the trigger.

'Bugger it! I've run out of caps.'

The other boy reappeared over the ridge and spat at the oak tree. He pointed towards the highest branches. 'Oy, big bollocks. Bet I can climb fucking higher than you can.'

This was answered with a tough guy, 'Fuck off. No you fucking can't,' followed by a well-practised footballer's gob as an aside.

'Fucking prove it then.'

The boy with the gun didn't want to admit to his fear of heights. He gestured towards the thicket. 'Hey! How 'bout goin' in there.'

'You fucking scared?'

'Course not. I just thought as we're not s'posed to go in there . . .'

'Who says?'

''S got barbed wire round. There's prob'ly traps in there. To catch rabbits.'

126

'We'll go in there afterwards. Let's climb the fucking tree first.'

Evans peered through a small opening in the undergrowth and saw the boys starting to climb. He knew he had to abandon his hiding place now, get out of the copse without being seen. But what if they spotted him? He had to decide quickly, before the boy who had the gun persuaded his friend to explore the wood.

He got into a crouching position and waited until the boys were out of sight, masked by the leaves of the oak. Then he stepped on each rung of the barbed wire fence and heaved himself over, catching his hand on one of the barbs.

'Come on,' cried one of the voices from the tree. 'I'm nearly at the top.'

Evans felt the wire tearing across the palm of his hand and the bushes shook behind him as the fence sprang back into place. He cursed his luck. Now he was at his most vulnerable, on the run in broad daylight. The only thing he could do was head south-west then double back once he was way out of sight. As he sprinted past the oak, he spotted the abandoned cap gun lying beneath the tree. He grabbed it and shoved it into his pocket.

Halfway up the tree, the owner of the gun, clinging for dear life to the main trunk, spotted Evans's retreating form. He stared uncertainly, wondering why the man was running. Then he alerted his friend much higher up.

'Gareth.'

'What?'

'Look at that man. Over there.'

'Where? I can't see no one.'

Evans bobbed out of sight. Seconds later he came into view again as he ran up the next hill.

'There. There he is,' insisted the boy who'd spotted him.

In the high branches, Gareth pushed the leaves aside and glimpsed Evans just as he disappeared over the top of

another hill. 'Blimey, Trevor. You're fucking right.' There
was a short pause while he tried to absorb what he'd seen,
and marry it to the recent events of the news. News that had
given him and Trevor endless pleasure as they fantasised
about escaped lunatics. They both made the connection at
the same moment.

'It might be the killer what's escaped from the loony bin.'

'I know. Shall we go home?'

'I don't wanna get down, Gar. I'm scared.'

'Yeah. Me too.'

Chapter 15

Lambert's car screeched to a halt outside the council house. A sad net curtain was tugged aside and a face peered out, round and wearing heavy make-up, peroxide hair like yellow straw. The curtain fell back into place with an angry movement. Lambert got out of the car and took in the neglected house at a glance. Grey pebble dash, paint peeling, no visible pride showing in any part of the property. The front garden was a patch of earth and a depository for old household appliances. As he walked up the uneven front path, neighbours standing in the doorway of the house next door stopped speaking and stared at him, unashamedly curious and a shade hostile.

He was about to knock when the door was thrown open aggressively by the blonde woman. She looked as if she was dressed to go out. Her figure was top heavy, but she had slim, firm dancer's legs and was wearing black tights and a short skirt, deliberately showing off her best feature. She clutched a packet of Marlboro Lights and a disposable gas lighter as if they'd been grafted onto her hand.

'About bloody time,' she snapped.

Lambert flipped open his ID. 'Mrs Powell? Can I have a word with your son?'

'I hope it's not going to take long. Only we've got to go out.'

'It's important, Mrs Powell. Life and death.'

'That's why it's taken you nearly an hour to get here.'

'I had to come from Swansea. Foot down all the way.'

She stared at him for a moment, deciding whether to relent or not, enjoying her brief moment of power.

'Sorry,' Lambert added. 'Traffic. It was unavoidable.'

Appeased, she inclined her head towards her front room. 'All right. But I've got to leave in ten minutes.'

Lambert stepped inside and the door slammed shut behind him. One of the next door neighbours shouted at the closed door, 'I wouldn't go in there, mister. She'll have the trousers off you.'

She and her friend laughed raucously.

*   *   *

Although he couldn't hear anything other than the wind sweeping across the hills, and the occasional bleating of sheep, Evans's instinct for self-preservation made him stop and listen, every fibre of his being alert. A feeling of imminent danger enveloped him. He remained frozen, tense and straining for every sound. But still he couldn't hear anything. Perhaps it was a sixth sense. He felt something was getting closer, and any minute now . . .

The only cover was a clump of gorse bushes. He dropped onto his stomach and crawled quickly into the thickest bush. He lay rigid, shutting his eyes tight against the pain he had to endure as dozens of sharp thorns pricked his flesh. Then he heard them approaching. His ear close to the ground, he listened to the heavy thud of their boots. Hardly daring to breathe, he tried to count the footsteps. At least a dozen and heading his way. As they neared his hiding place, their footsteps getting louder and louder, he began to shiver and broke out in a feverish sweat. And he felt angry. Angry that he might be caught in this dishonourable way, like a cowering animal, unable to defend himself. He could hear the boots up close, almost upon him. Then one of them brushed past his hiding place and the bush crackled and swished. He heard a female voice and a laugh. Then the footsteps carried on by, and he heard the last of them receding into the distance. Curiosity got the better of him, and he risked peering from a gap in the bush. He saw a group of ramblers disappearing over the brow of a hill. Once again thanked his luck. Had it been a police search party, he'd have stood no chance.

He waited a good ten minutes before emerging from his hiding place and continuing his journey northwards. Once over the next hillock he found what he was looking for. A giant stone, standing about ten feet high, holding court over a small circle of stones in a dip in the mountainside, indiscernible from a distance. The large stone had strange designs cut into the side of it, and it was believed that this spot was once the site of human sacrifice. He knew he was heading in the right direction now. Just beyond the rocky promontory to the north were some caves, going deep into the mountainside. He could hide there until nightfall.

Taking a final look at the monolith, he squinted up at it, paying homage to his ancestors, imagining how these pre-Christian Celts killed their sacrificial victims. Without thinking, he took the cap gun from his pocket and examined it. Not a bad replica for a toy. A small automatic, like a Falcon.

Even though it was fake, he felt like a soldier again. A warrior.

*　　　　*　　　　*

Lambert had to compete with a Tom and Jerry cartoon blaring from the widescreen TV set that dominated the chaotic room. Two boys sat on a sofa, eating chips and battered sausages from a mess of paper strewn across a coffee table.

'Hello,' Lambert greeted them. 'Which one of you is Trevor?'

'He is,' said the youngest of the boys disappointedly, wishing he had been the one to spot the escaped lunatic.

Lambert pulled up a chair next to the oldest boy, who stared disconsolately at his bag of chips, clearly worried about something. Lambert glanced at his watch and spoke to him gently.

'Trevor, why didn't you tell your mother about this man earlier?'

Trevor's shifty eyes darted to his mother, then to Lambert. 'I didn't wanna get in no trouble.'

'Why would you have got into trouble, Trevor?'

His mother loomed over the coffee table and stabbed a finger at him accusingly. ''Cos he knows he ain't s'posed to go down that side of the village, that's why. 'Cos of them pikeys.'

'What made you tell your mum when you did, then?'

Trevor stared at his brother contemptuously before answering. ''Cos John grassed me up.'

'He saw the man on the telly,' the youngest boy told Lambert, as if this explanation squared it with his brother.

Lambert leaned forward towards Trevor. 'Listen, Trevor,' he began, allowing just the right amount of urgency to creep into his voice. 'Think you can remember the direction the man took? If I were to take you to the spot where you saw him . . .'

Their mother interrupted. 'But we're going out. It's my boyfriend's birthday. We gorra leave in ten minutes.'

She snatched a chip off the table and rammed it into her mouth.

'Mrs Powell, I can't begin to stress the importance of finding this man before he . . .'

'All right,' Mrs Powell barked through a mouthful of chip. She rounded on her son. 'You little sod. Why couldn't you say something earlier?'

Lambert rose. 'Come on then, Trevor. If you'd like to come with us, Mrs Powell.'

Mrs Powell gave him a dismissive wave, like brushing a

fly away, and lit up a cigarette. 'No thanks. I'd better phone Wayne. He don't like to be kept waiting.'

'Can I come?' asked John, his voice suddenly bright.

Lambert looked towards his mother. 'I've no objections, Mrs Powell.'

'Oh, for Christ's sake. Don't be long then.'

The boys shot to their feet. Trevor grabbed a handful of chips and said, 'I hope my cap gun's still there.'

They left the house, the boys feeling important and swaggering, pleased the gossiping neighbours were witnesses to their moment of glory. The neighbours watched with suspicion and envy, itching with curiosity. The boys argued over who should sit in the front and Lambert told them both to sit in the back. They drove through the silent village, turned into a steep hill, on which stood a forbidding grey chapel that was like an old warship frozen in time, and climbed the winding, narrow road for about a quarter of a mile until they reached a farm.

'This is as far as we can go by car,' Trevor said.

Lambert parked where the road was wide enough for another car to pass and they continued across the fields on foot. As soon as he spotted the oak tree, Trevor and his brother ran excitedly towards it, Trevor shouting, 'There it is. That's the tree. That's where we saw him.' As soon as Lambert caught up with the boys at the bottom of the tree, he asked Trevor which way the man was running. Trevor pointed south-west. Lambert frowned thoughtfully.

'You're sure?'

'Yeah. Me an' Gareth spotted him from up there. He was running that way.'

John gave his brother a friendly shove and started to climb the tree. 'Bet I can get higher than you.'

Trevor grabbed him by the collar and pulled him back.

'Hey!' he protested.

'Not now. We've gorra get back or Mum'll kill us.' Trevor

133

scanned the ground hastily. 'It's gone. Some fucker's nicked my gun.'

Angered by his brother's roughness, John rubbed his neck and said, 'And I'm going to tell her you've been swearing.'

Trevor grabbed his wrist and started to give him a Chinese burn.

'No, I won't tell her. Honest I won't.'

Lambert, lost in thought, stared in the direction in which Evans had run off. 'What's your game, soldier boy?' he muttered. 'What makes you tick?'

The boys studied him curiously, then looked at each other and giggled.

'By the way, Trevor,' Lambert said. 'What did this man look like?'

Trevor stopped giggling and looked guilty, as if he'd been told off.

'I couldn't see him up close. He was runnin' away. But I'm sure it was the man off the telly.'

'What was he wearing?'

'Um. One of those coats. Anorak, like.'

'What colour?'

'Dark. Couldn't really see the colour. But he had soldier's trousers.'

'Camouflaged?'

Trevor nodded. 'I'm sure it's him,' he said, fervently.

'You've been a great help, Trevor. Thanks.'

Feeling left out, Trevor's young brother asked, 'D'you think you'll catch him, mister?'

'Oh yes, we'll catch him all right.'

'You going to take him alive or shoot him?'

This was something Lambert hadn't really considered. 'Alive, of course,' he answered without conviction.

The boy's face crumpled with disappointment. 'Oh.'

'Right,' said Lambert. 'I'll run you both home.'

As they walked back towards the car, Lambert felt his sleeve being tugged.

'Will I get a reward if you catch him?' Trevor looked up at the detective, his dark eyes wide and appealing, begging like a puppy dog.

'If it's him what helps catch him,' said the younger brother, smacking his fist into his palm, 'he ought to get at least five quid.'

Lambert stopped and rummaged through his pockets. 'I can't argue with that,' he said.

A greedy glint surfaced in Trevor's eyes and his brother got over-excited and circled whirring round the two of them, arms spread out like the wings of a plane.

Lambert gave Trevor a crumpled five-pound note and gave his brother two pound coins. 'That's for coming along to assist us,' he told him.

The money vanished into their pockets and neither of them thanked him. As he drove them home, he cast his mind back to when Natasha had been about three years old. Helen had become pregnant again and he had hoped they might have a boy this time. The perfect family. Then came the miscarriage. And Helen had never been able to conceive again. Was this when things started to go wrong? He had always been faithful to her up until this time. Then, after the miscarriage, she lost interest in sex; and it seemed as if she was merely obliging him by going through the motions once a month when she felt up to it. Now, tired of always shouldering the burden of guilt, he projected some of the blame of their broken marriage onto Helen. But the truth was, he had turned to other women because Helen had provided him with an excuse, like an alcoholic hitting the bottle big time on receiving bad news.

A squeal from the back seat jerked him out of his introspective mood.

'OK, pack it in,' he told them. 'We're here.'

Their mother stood at the door, seething with impatience. As he let them out, he gave her a wave; but she just glared, dragged the children indoors and slammed the door. He drove on for a hundred yards, parked and switched off the engine, then called Superintendent Phillips on his mobile. Trying to keep the gloating tone out of his voice, he told him about the boy's description of the man they saw running away from the oak tree. Phillips, full of blustering self-confidence, denied the possibility that Evans might have slipped through the net, as Lambert guessed he would, and questioned the reliability of the boy's eyewitness account, saying that it was probably just another of a long list of false sightings. Lambert stressed the importance of searching the area, especially as there was still some daylight left. He told Phillips the boy had given an accurate description of Evans, without being prompted. Reluctantly, the superintendent concurred, saying that he would send some men down to have a look around. Lambert asked if he could be informed if they found anything, and Phillips, who had only agreed to the search to cover his own back, ended the conversation on a dubious, pessimistic note.

'I still think it's a waste of bloody time. And eyewitness accounts are notoriously unreliable.'

Irritated, Lambert clicked his mobile off and headed back towards Swansea.

Chapter 16

Two nights with hardly any sleep resulted in Lambert starting to feel the effects physically, in a way which was worrying. A pain shot through the left side of his body if he raised his arm or twisted it into a certain position, and he immediately began thinking the worst. He told himself he was just being neurotic; he had slept for a few hours last night scrunched up in the back of the car. No wonder he ached. He needed to relax; lie soaking in a nice hot bath. He decided to call it a day and head for home.

Home! Not by any stretch of the imagination, he told himself.

As he drove back to Swansea, the night descended without warning over the hills, as if a stage curtain had been lowered. Lambert couldn't get Evans out of his mind. He knew the mercenary would be on his way now, secure in the cloak of night. But if Evans travelled at night, how come he'd been spotted by Trevor and his friend? And why was he now heading south-west, which was where he was heading earlier on, only this time he was further back and would have to cover more ground to get to where he wanted to go? None of it made sense, but it occupied Lambert's mind until he arrived back at his flat. As soon as he was indoors, the first thing he did was to check his answerphone. But no one had rung. Not a single social call, friend or family. Feeling lonely and washed out, he ran a bath, then poured himself a large gin and tonic. But even the tonic had lost its sparkle. While he waited for his bath to run, he gave Ellis a quick call for an update. He was told that Wallace had caught a virus, a stomach bug which was doing the rounds, and had gone home hours ago. And Ellis had encountered so much

137

red tape trying to get the information about the blood groups that Lambert told him to call it a day and make a fresh start the following morning. Before ringing off, Ellis asked if there was any news of Evans.

'Looks like he was heading south-west according to the kid who spotted him. Same direction as before, only now he's behind our men.'

'Cunning bastard,' Ellis said admiringly. 'You've got to hand it to the man. So what happens now? They all turn round and head north-east?'

Seeing the comic potential of the situation, Lambert laughed. 'Like a Buster Keaton film I saw. Backwards and forwards. It would drive Phillips mad. He still doesn't like to admit Evans could have broken through his search party.'

'What d'you reckon the chances are of catching him tonight?'

'Who knows. But even if they do catch him tonight, I still want that information tomorrow, Tony.'

Lambert's mobile rang.

'I've got to go. And my bath's overflowing. See you tomorrow.'

Grabbing his mobile, he dashed into the bathroom and turned the taps off before answering it. There was a short pause. Then Phillips, trying to sound as if humble-pie eating was never an option for people who had to get on with the job, told him they'd found a matching footprint confirming the boy's story, and that Evans must somehow have managed to evade the police and was now heading south-west again. Lambert grinned mischievously at his steamy reflection over the wash basin and wished Phillips luck.

*   *   *

Tuesday and still no sign of Evans. Lambert spent most of the day in the office, reading Evans's letters to Gwyneth Chandler; but, in spite of going over them and sifting through each detail, making notes as he went along, he discovered nothing that seemed relevant or that he didn't already know. And he couldn't make up his mind whether the young mercenary really believed all the guff he wrote about Celtic mysticism or whether he was just stringing her along to get the information he needed. After reading through them three or four times, he eventually came to the conclusion that it could be a combination of both. Perhaps Evans truly believed in the arcane mysteries of the Celts but was also using this knowledge as a means to an end.

Late afternoon, Ellis bounded into the office. Lambert looked up expectantly, and he knew Ellis had got a result by the way he stood grinning, savouring the moment. This is what Lambert always did himself at such moments, but in others he found it irritating.

'All right. Don't overdo it. What have you got?'

Ellis flipped open his notebook and consulted it, though he knew it off by heart. 'Evans's mother was blood group A. Ted Wilson was AB. But Ben Evans was group O. And Gary Evans was born on the 4th of April 1969. But his mother didn't leave Tregaron until late November '68. And she didn't meet Ben Evans until December that year.'

They stared expressionlessly at each other. There was a hint of a smile in Ellis's eyes as he saw the truth hit home.

'Shit!' Lambert exclaimed. 'You realise who Evans probably killed, don't you?'

Ellis, who had already worked it out, nodded. 'It doesn't bear thinking about. Not with my chapel upbringing. Oh yes, and another thing. Evans's mother was the Tregaron Carnival Queen in July 1968.'

*   *   *

Helen lay soaking in the bath. She had forgotten to pull the roller blind down and she could see the shadows of the trees through the frosted glass of the window, swaying and weaving a ghostly dance, and through the reflected images of the bathroom she thought she could see faces peering at her from the dark. She shut them out of her mind, ran some more hot water, then lay back again. She started to think of *him*. At first random images. The way he threw back his head and laughed; his face lit up and grinning proudly at her side while she breastfed Natasha; his breath on her shoulder as he massaged sun-tan lotion into her on the beach at Rhossili Bay. But gradually the images started to slip away and she began to wonder if he had been faithful to her all those years ago, before Natasha was born. And what about when she was pregnant with Natasha? Had he been screwing some bit of stuff on the side then?

She shivered, chased the repugnant thought from her mind, sat up abruptly and reached for the towel. As she did, she caught sight of herself in the full-length mirror. Her face was flushed now from the steamy heat, but it glowed with a renewed energy. For so long, ever since his infidelities had come to light, she had thought of herself as worthless and unattractive. But gradually she stopped blaming herself. She stopped caring about his infidelities, and realised it was nothing to do with her. It was just the way he was. It didn't excuse anything. But at least she was able to look in the mirror again without feeling she had become old and ugly. And as the distance grew between them, her awareness of how much he still wanted her increased. She would never have him back, but it was comforting to know that he still loved her, only now she was the one who was in command of the situation.

She stepped out of the bath and began to dry herself. She was struck by a sudden irony. The pragmatic ex-husband, the doubter, the non-believer, turning to her for help in unravelling ley line mysteries. Perhaps it had little to do with the investigation. Maybe it was just his way of keeping in contact with her. An umbilical cord; a line of string winding through a dark labyrinth, bonding them together, like an invisible ley line.

She stared at her reflection and froze as sudden realisation sent messages screaming through her brain like electric currents. She knew what was wrong with those charts. She dried herself hurriedly, knowing she had the answer now. God! The hours she had spent poring over those charts. And it was so simple. A child could have seen it.

She threw on her bathrobe and dashed downstairs.

Chapter 17

Night was descending rapidly. Gwyneth Chandler stood at the back door and tapped the side of the cat food tin with a fork.

'Bran! Bran!' she called. Her voice had a disappointed, slightly desperate edge to it. She was feeling lonely. She missed her daughters, and the company of the family pet in the evenings was a comfort. But the cat had slept all day in front of the fire and was now nowhere to be seen. She tried pursing her lips, making a high-pitched squishing sound which sometimes did the trick. There was a rustle of leaves from a bush nearby, but this turned out to be a large blackbird. She sighed disappointedly and watched the bird hopping about in its search for food. From the living room came the budgie-like cheep from her telephone. She placed the cat food and fork on the work surface and dashed into the living room to answer it. She thought it might be Bethan and Gwen ringing her from Canada. They had rung at this time yesterday. Her spirits rose as she picked up the phone and gave the number. But her hopes were immediately dashed as there was a slight pause, followed by a mumbled apology. A wrong number. She sighed with frustration, hung up without speaking, and poured herself another red wine. She had drunk two glasses already. And she had drunk an entire bottle last night. Now it looked as if she would get through another bottle tonight. She frowned, feeling guilty, and wondered if she was becoming an alcoholic. Then she dismissed the idea, thinking it was only for this week until her daughters came home. She took her drink over to the fireplace and settled into the armchair, leaned forward and put another log on the fire. It crackled comfortingly. It was homely and cosy, but she was bored. She would have given

142

anything to get out the house for tonight, go for a meal with someone in the town, instead of just sitting here . . .

'Bugger it!' she exclaimed loudly, immediately regretting having said it for the way it accentuated the silence. She picked up the ley line charts from where she had left them on the floor by the chair, and began to study them again. These were copies of the ones she had sent to Gary Evans when he was at that hospital. She thought about him now, as she had the previous night, trying to imagine him on the run, crashing through the countryside. She stared at one of the lines, following it up with her finger to where the small prehistoric circle of stones on the hill behind her cottage stood. She shivered involuntarily and her stomach fluttered and heaved. She felt vulnerable. Tense and straining for every sound from outside the cottage, she thought she heard a small squeaking noise that sounded like the scuff of a rubber soul on concrete. She rose hurriedly, turned the big iron key in the lock and leaned back against the door, consoled by the thought that although she was behaving ridiculously, she wasn't taking any chances either. But when she felt the cold draught blowing through from the kitchen, she realised she had left the back door wide open. She hurried through to the kitchen, desperately wishing that Bran would come in. Through the open doorway she saw that it was dark outside now. She grabbed the door and swung it closed. As it slammed shut, from the corner of her eye she saw him. Her stomach lurched, discordant screams of terror pierced her brain, and as she gulped frantically for air, a hard, calloused hand clapped over her mouth, cutting off her breath. She was pulled roughly backwards against his body and she felt cold steel pressing against her throat. She wanted to cry. She wondered if this was how it was going to end. She felt his lips against her ear, whispering urgently,

'Don't scream. Don't make a sound.'

*   *   *

143

When Helen opened the door in her bathrobe, Lambert stood in the porch gazing at her like a lovesick adolescent. She pretended not to notice and stood aside, inviting him in. As he entered, she said,

'God! You stink of smoke. Some things never change.'

She saw him staring at the coat rack below the stairs.

'There isn't anyone else, you know.' She thought she saw the beginnings of a self-satisfied smile tugging at the corners of his mouth, so added forcefully, 'Not yet.'

'What did you want to show me?' he said.

'In here.'

Helen led the way into the living room. She was about to show him the ley line charts but noticed he was rooted to the spot, staring at her. His face was blank. It was hard to tell what he was thinking.

'What?' she said.

Then he smiled slowly, giving her that eye twinkle that he seemed capable of turning on at will.

'I hope you haven't just showered and rubbed yourself in exotic oils for my benefit.'

Without thinking, she moved a little closer to him.

'Don't flatter yourself.'

Her voice was husky. She felt she was losing control, sliding towards the inevitable. Pull yourself together, she thought. Don't be a fool. His arms slipped around her waist. She knew she should have resisted but felt powerless, knowing that it was something she wanted to happen and it was of her own choosing.

'You smell gorgeous,' he said, his voice a degree softer, melodious.

She giggled. 'Which is more than can be said for someone not a million miles from here.'

'I'm sorry. I came straight from the pub.'

'No! I'd never have guessed.'

'If you like, I could pop upstairs and take a shower. Or I could run us a bath. Just like old times.'

'I think I'm clean enough.'

'Who said anything about washing?'

'Fancy yourself, don't you.'

He pressed himself closer to her. She could feel the bulge pressing through her bathrobe.

'No, it's you I fancy. Can't you tell?'

'You'd feel like this with any old scrubber you picked up.'

'Not like this I wouldn't.' His voice dropped to a whisper. 'Oh, Helen . . .'

'Oh, Harry,' she mimicked.

'Stop teasing. You always were a bit of a PT.'

She tilted her face up towards his. 'Ah, but I always delivered in the end.'

It flashed through his head that the opposite had been nearer the truth. But as he looked deep into her eyes, indulging in the briefest anticipation of the kiss, he brushed the past to one side, seeing only the possibility of a new beginning.

He kissed her gently on the lips and slowly her mouth opened to receive his tongue.

*   *   *

Gwyneth's mouth tasted of dry fear. She could feel the cold steel pressed hard against her throat. She wanted to swallow but was afraid to move a muscle.

'I'm not going to hurt you. Understand?'

His voice was softer now, less desperate, trying to put her at ease.

'But I don't want you to scream. If I take my hand away, you won't scream?'

145

She shook her head as much as she could in his smothering hold.

'Right. I'm going to take my hand away.'

The strong smell of earth and grass on his fingers vanished as her mouth was released from his iron grip. He took the blade away from her throat and she saw that it was nothing more than a pen-knife. And he'd been holding the blunt side of it against her skin. Perhaps he meant what he said about not harming her. She eased her body away from his and turned round. She was panting now, as the sudden adrenalin rush left her feeling drained and shaky. She stared straight into his eyes. They were clear, pale blue. He held her gaze then folded the blade of the pen-knife shut without looking at it.

'You OK?' he asked. The knife vanished into his pocket.

Her throat was parched from fear. She licked her lips and swallowed saliva before answering hoarsely, 'I think so.'

He tilted his head slightly in the direction of the door to the living room. 'Mind if we go and sit down? I've had it. I'm knackered.'

She led the way and he followed closely behind her. He cast his eyes round the room until they alighted on the phone on the occasional table by the window. He went over and unplugged the jack from the socket. When he straightened up, he saw the desperate look in her eyes and he felt sorry for her. He wanted to reassure her. Perhaps he could do this by making her feel special, by telling her she was the only living person now who could possibly understand him. But he couldn't. Not just yet. Instead, his voice little more than a whisper, he said:

'I told you. It's OK. I'm not going to hurt you.'

'It's not that. It's my daughters. They're in Canada – with their father. They might ring.'

He shrugged. 'I can't risk it. They'll just get a ringing tone. They'll think you're out. I'm sorry.'

Gwyneth stared at him, keeping her expression neutral. Had he meant it about not harming her? Why had he come here? Was it because of her letters? She regretted writing to him now. She should never have become involved. He smiled slightly. It was almost imperceptible, but it was there. She was sure of it. Putting her at ease?

'I'm sorry,' he repeated, his voice soft and sympathetic.

They stared at each other across the room, the dining table between them. She wondered if she should make a break for it, into the kitchen and out of the back door. It was only a matter of twenty yards to her nearest neighbour's cottage. Perhaps not even that far. Her eyes wavered, flickered slightly towards the kitchen. She saw his eyes follow hers and knew he could see the thought running through her head.

'I knew you'd come here,' she blurted out. It was a lie. She wondered why she'd said it. Perhaps it was to reassure him, make him think they were on the same wavelength. But he took it the wrong way.

'You haven't called the police?'

She shook her head. 'No.'

'Why not? If you knew I was coming here, why didn't you call them?'

She hesitated. 'I don't know. I . . . I didn't think there was any need. I know you've killed someone, but I don't think you're a violent man, Gary.'

She could have kicked herself. It had sounded patronising, as if she was trying to humour him.

'Taking a bit of a risk though, aren't you?'

'Suppose I am. But our relationship, our letters – meant a great deal to me.'

He nodded slowly, and she saw the present of his eyes vanish to the past, sifting through the shadows for some significant echoes from a primitive existence. Something mystical. And, as if to confirm her thoughts, he muttered:

147

'Destiny.'

She waited for him to elaborate, aware of her heart pounding out an ancient drum beat and of a strange high-pitched electronic humming inside her head. She stared closely at him, searching for any small clue that he might have been saying it for effect. But his unblinking gaze remained distant.

'What did you mean,' she said, 'by "destiny"?'

Slowly, his eyes sought hers again. 'Nothing,' he said. 'I'm tired.'

She saw him glance at the wine bottle.

'Would you like a drink?'

He nodded. 'I could murder one.'

Gwyneth felt a cold hand brushing her spine at the unfortunate choice of words. She told herself not to be so stupid. It was only an expression. She was sure he had meant nothing by it. She got another glass from the dresser and filled it with wine. As she approached him, she noticed his eyes had softened and he seemed calm, sympathetic, trying to show he cared for her; wanting her on his side. Their fingers touched briefly as he took the glass and she felt a slight thrill, the sensual butterfly touch of nervous would-be lovers, a touch that was tantalisingly significant. Had he felt the same? Or had she imagined a chemistry that was entirely one-sided? It was absurd. Held hostage by a ruthless killer and she starts imagining the beginnings of a romance. Behaving like an irrational teenager. Been watching too many films.

She fetched her glass from beside the fireplace and topped it up. Then she asked him, 'Have you eaten?' Calmly. Matter-of-fact. Just as if he was her partner home late from work.

'Long time ago,' he replied.

She smiled, feeling safer in his company now. 'I expect you could eat a scabby horse, hooves an' all.'

He stared at her for some time and she wondered if her reply had confused him. She became aware of the clock ticking on the mantlepiece and a sheep bleating far away. Time had gone into slow motion, every action and thought was sharp and clear but unreal. Eventually he smiled. There was irony in the expression, as if he too saw how ludicrous this cosy, domestic situation was.

'I expect I could,' he agreed. 'I'm starving.'

'I'll go and see what I can cook you.'

As she started towards the door, she noticed the sharp, keen glint in his eyes and froze.

'I'm not going to dash out into the night screaming for help. Something tells me I wouldn't get very far. You can come out to the kitchen with me, if you like.'

He seemed to relax then and followed her out. She lit the gas under the deep fryer, took four large potatoes from the vegetable rack and began to peel them over the sink.

'Pile of chips and a cheese omelette do you?'

'Yes. Thanks.'

Evans stood and watched her, admiring her shape in the tightness of her denims. From the corner of her eye she became aware of his interest and wondered how she would cope if he tried to force himself on her. But somehow he didn't seem to be the rapist type. And what is the rapist type? she asked herself.

'You don't have to worry,' he assured her. 'I've never taken a woman by force.'

As if he could read her mind.

She turned, looked deep into his eyes, and in that flickering instant they both knew. If he wanted her tonight, she would say yes. Yes and yes again, just like Molly Bloom.

*   *   *

As he began to unbutton his shirt, Lambert glanced apprehensively around the bedroom for evidence of change. There was none that he could see. It was exactly the way he remembered it. Yet it felt peculiar. Different. He couldn't pin it down. He sat on the edge of the bed and slipped his socks and trousers off. Then he realised why it felt so strange. It was her bedroom, and hers alone. He was history. No. Not even history. He'd been airbrushed out of it.

He felt nervous. His stomach danced tremulously, reminding him of their first time together. He felt excited, much too excited, by the memory, and he prayed that he wasn't going to disappoint her. Then she came in from the bathroom. She had stripped off completely and her body glowed in the light from the bedside lamp. Her legs were still attractively firm and slim. He stood up as she came towards him and slid his arms around her waist. God! How soft she felt. He'd forgotten just how good it was. His throat clammed up. He felt like an awkward teenager again. She looked into his eyes. Hers were smiling, aware of his predicament. He cleared his throat softly before speaking.

'It's been a while since . . .'

Her eyebrows rose quizzically, almost mockingly, waiting for him to continue.

'Since I've had sex,' he lied. It wasn't as if she had asked about any other women he'd been with since they had parted, so why did he feel it was necessary to lie? Perhaps it was because he wanted Helen to believe he'd been behaving himself, deliberately saving himself for a night such as this.

'Why are you telling me this?' she asked, a trace of suspicion in her voice.

'Well – I hope I don't disappoint you.'

'Oh, God! The ego of the man,' she laughed. 'Worried about his performance.'

*   *   *

Gwyneth sat across the table from Evans and watched as he swallowed the last mouthful of food.

'You were hungry.'

His knife and fork clattered onto the plate. He looked up at her expectantly. Almost like a little boy waiting for his pudding, she thought. She smiled back at him.

'So what happens now?'

He shrugged and remained silent.

'You know, I worked it out from the ley lines where you were heading. And if I can work it out, so can the police.'

'I don't think so. At least, not for a while.'

She raised her eyebrows questioningly, soliciting an explanation.

Smiling confidently, he said, 'I altered the maps. Changed them. It'll take them some time to put two and two together.'

Like a stomach-churning roller coaster drop, her heart swooped fearfully. The effect of his words must have shown, because he frowned understandingly and reached across the table and patted her hand reassuringly.

'Don't worry. I'm not going to hurt you.'

The touch of his hand was brief. But it was instinctive, signifying the habitual tactility of a long-standing relationship, like a mother and son. She swallowed before she spoke. It seemed loud and intrusive in the clock-ticking silence.

'You've been through a great deal, Gary. What are you searching for?'

'Nothing. What makes you think I'm searching for anything?'

'Because of what you said in your letters. All that stuff about the Celtic Otherworld.'

Embarrassed, he dropped his eyes. 'Well, that was just . . .'

'Stringing me along? To get the ley line charts?'

He shrugged slightly, pursing his lips, unable to look her in the eye. 'Maybe.'

151

'Can I ask you something?'

He remained silent, his face deadpan, so she asked him anyway.

'How many men have you killed? I don't mean the farmer. I mean when you were in the SAS.'

'I don't know. Dozens. Maybe more. I lost count.'

'And did you feel any –'

'Guilt?' He shook his head. 'They were soldiers. You live by the sword, you die by the sword.'

'These soldiers you killed, presumably in Northern Ireland, were fighting for a cause. What's your cause, Gary? Who are you fighting for?'

She saw him inwardly struggling against her question, searching for an answer.

'I'm a soldier,' he murmured after a long pause. 'It's what I do.'

'Did you have a girlfriend? A lover? Someone special?'

'Not permanent, like. I'm not queer, if that's what you mean.'

She laughed, stood up and started to clear his plate. 'No, I'm not suggesting you are.'

As she moved close to him, her thigh brushed against his arm. Her nerves were sharpened by the sensation, and the touch of their bodies was like warm soothing water. She felt his hand moving gently over her buttocks and he tugged her towards him, letting his head sink into the contours of her thighs and stomach. She put the dinner plate back onto the table and ran her fingers through his close-cropped hair. She felt the heat from his hands on her thighs and the sensation startled her. She caught her breath, realising she was being swept along helplessly, giving in to her instinct and pleasure. For the briefest of moments, she questioned her actions, wondered if she was hurling herself into the most dangerous of encounters. But already she seemed to have passed the point of no return. There was no going back now.

152

'If you want,' she whispered, 'we could go upstairs to bed.'

He took his head away from her lap and looked up at her. How young he seemed. She was at least fifteen years older than him.

'I've been on the run for three nights now. During the day I've been sleeping rough. I probably smell.'

She smiled and ruffled his fine hair like she would a little boy.

'You smell of nature and the wild.'

'Even so: I'd like to take a bath first.'

The request reassured her, made her feel safe.

Chapter 18

Lambert lay propped against the pillow, Helen curled up close beside him. Her face looked peaceful, like a child's, reminding him of Natasha. He wanted so desperately to give his daughter a home to which she could occasionally return, but he knew it was too late. There would be no duty-bound visits on Christmas Day any more. He had given Natasha the excuse she needed to stay at her boyfriend's parents during the festive season. They were respectable, middle class, and lived in a large house in a trendy part of Barnes in south-west London. The boyfriend's father was the head teacher of an expensive preparatory school and his mother was a harpist. They were a family of five, the three children growing up fast, all artistic and all would no doubt be successful. A devoted, perfect family. Unlike his own upbringing. His father a cowboy builder, boozy and lecherous. Lambert becoming a copper hadn't gone down well with the old man at first, but at least he felt he could change his life for the better. But the change was superficial. Beneath the surface, he was just as bad as the old man. Worse, probably. It was like Melanie had pointed out: he was the charmer, the smooth operator, that kills through love.

His eyes suddenly moistened with small tears of self-pity. His shame and his guilt heightened his loss, the empty feeling that nothing would ever be the same again. He looked down at Helen and stroked her hair gently. She moaned softly, blinked sleep from her eyes and stretched her legs out like a cat uncurling itself.

'What time is it?'

'Early.'

She pulled herself into a sitting position, plumped the pillows, then lay back against them, exhausted by the effort.

'How early?' she demanded, irritation creeping into her voice.

'Half six.'

'Couldn't you sleep?'

'Couple of hours maybe. I've been awake for ages. Been thinking about us.'

She stared straight ahead. She could guess what was coming and braced herself for it.

'Sweetheart?' He wanted her to look at him, to see the tears in his eyes before they dried up. They were so insignificant, though. Would she notice them?

'The answer's no.'

Helen could feel his eyes boring into her and pictured his affronted, puzzled expression, the one that used to make her laugh all those years ago, but now she found irritating.

'I don't understand,' he emphasised slowly.

'I can still fancy you, can't I?'

'Yes, but . . .'

'It wouldn't work. I think I still love you. But it's hopeless.' She turned her face towards him and hit him harder with the next sentence. 'You won't ever change.'

'I can try.'

'Try's not good enough, Harry. It's too late. Can't you get that through your thick policeman's skull?'

Lambert sighed gently. He thought about moving closer to her, holding her tight and perhaps trying to make love to her again. But somehow the extravagant mood of the night had disappeared, leaving him with a fumbling awkwardness he hadn't felt since the loss of his virginity. To compensate for the stilted atmosphere, he chuckled and said,

'We sort of got sidetracked last night. What was it you rang about?'

She threw him a sideways look. 'Getting back on the job, are you? That's if you were ever off it.'

'Seriously.'

'Those ley line maps Evans had. They were fake.'

'What?'

Suddenly alert now, Lambert shifted in the bed. His knee came in contact with Helen's thigh.

'Ouch!'

'What do you mean they were fake?'

'They were photocopies. And they've been changed. I compared them to some others I found. You know those books of Natasha's? She's got loads of stuff about Celtic legends and . . .'

'Yes, yes, yes,' Lambert said impatiently, his eyes ablaze with excitement. 'And?'

'Well, Evans must have had access to a photocopier because some of the ancient stone circles going north have been eliminated.'

Lambert swung his legs out of bed and grabbed his underpants from the floor where he'd dropped them.

'Show me. Quickly.'

*   *   *

Gwyneth watched Gary Evans as he lay sleeping. She was tormented by a fear buried deep inside, a fear that remained disturbingly out of reach. What was it? If only she could bring it to the surface, she might be able to deal with it. But her brain was cluttered by random thoughts and memories that skipped about in a disorderly fashion. She thought of her schooldays. Her first fumbling love affair. Memories of places, of sunsets and castles. She was a romantic. A sensualist and a pantheist. In love with nature. So what was she doing making love to a trained killer? A man who thought no more about blowing out another man's brains than someone swatting a fly. Yet he'd been a considerate lover. And she found the notion of attentive lover and ruthless killer highly disturbing.

He'd spent ages in the bathroom preparing himself. He even borrowed her delicate razor and shaved his three-day growth several times before he seemed satisfied with the smoothness. When he eventually did slip quietly beneath the duvet, he held her tight, and kissed her slowly and gently, taking his time. He knew what he was doing and did all the right things for her. But there was something coldly efficient about his lovemaking: a trained expert going through the motions. When they climaxed together, she cried out with agonising pleasure; but he remained silent, clenching his teeth.

He opened his eyes suddenly, as if he'd been pretending to be asleep. She reached out and stroked his cheek.

'Gary,' she said softly. 'Thank you for last night. But.'

'But?' he questioned as he sat up.

'What happens now?'

He ignored the question. His glazed look accentuated the silence.

'Gary, if there's anything you want to tell me, I promise I won't . . . I'll keep it to myself. I promise.'

'Confession time, like? Good for the soul and that?'

'Well – it might help. Help you to come to terms with everything. That farmer, Gary. Who was he?'

'I never knew him. Never. He was just flesh and blood, that's all.'

A beat. Somewhere in her subconscious she had known all along. It had been lying beneath the surface, waiting for the trigger that would unleash the horror of his crime. It was like a stinging slap.

'My God! He was your father, wasn't he? You killed your own father.'

Apart from a nervous tic in his cheek, Evans's face showed no emotion.

'He raped my mother. The bastard raped her. She never reported it. She came to live in Swansea and married my stepfather. For years I thought he was my real father.'

'What was he like? Your Stepfather?'

'Want me to quote Exodus, chapter and verse? Or Jeremiah? A good beating can do wonders for the memory. I had to have it word perfect for the bastard.'

Gwyneth leant towards him, kissed his forehead tenderly and squeezed his hand. 'Poor Gary. It sounds as if he was . . . mentally unstable. It's hard to believe bible-thumping bigots like that still exist. When did you discover he wasn't your real father?'

'He was killed in an accident. Or maybe it wasn't an accident.'

'What d'you mean?'

'He was a roofer. Maybe someone he worked with gave him the elbow.' Evans laughed bitterly. 'That's what I'd have done.'

'So that's when your mother told you he was really your stepfather.'

'It let me off the hook. Saved me having to attend the funeral. I celebrated with me mates instead. Champagne all round.'

'What else did your mother tell you? Did she tell you who your real father was?'

Evans shook his head. 'She told me about the rape. But she wouldn't tell me who he was. I think she knew what I'd do.'

'How did you find out eventually?'

'As she was dying, she told me his name. And the name of the farm.'

'Why did she do that, d'you think?'

'Maybe she wanted revenge after all. Human nature.'

'So you took it. For her and for you.'

'I couldn't go through with it,' he said, his voice rising in anger. 'All those years of training, freeing the mind of emotion, and I couldn't go through with it.'

'Gary, are you telling me you *didn't* kill him?'

He looked deep into her eyes and said, 'Oh, I killed him all right. I killed him.'

*   *   *

'See the faint smudges on the photocopy,' said Helen. 'It looks as if he Tipp-Exed over the originals, then photo-copied them.'

Lambert stared hard at the map laid out across the coffee table. 'No, I can't see anything.'

'I think you've reached that age when you need to wear reading glasses.'

'There's nothing wrong with my eyesight.'

'Well, you'll just have to take my word for it then.' Helen stabbed her index finger at a spot on the map. 'These ancient sites have been erased, so have these ley lines. Have a look at the same spot in Natasha's book.'

Lambert felt his stomach lurch. 'Christ! These lines go north.'

'Exactly,' agreed Helen. 'Up to this ancient site outside Aberystwyth. D'you suppose that's where he's heading?'

But Lambert wasn't listening to her. He snatched the telephone and began dialling furiously. 'Mind if I use your phone?'

'Help yourself.'

*   *   *

Evans sat upright in bed, watching the brightness of the day growing behind the thin curtains. Gwyneth knew it was borrowed time now.

'Gary,' she began tentatively, her voice tremulous and small. 'I'm sure if they knew why you killed him . . . about your mother . . . and the rape . . . and what it's done to you . . .'

Evans interrupted her. 'No. I'm not going back to that . . . asylum.'

159

'You might not have to. That's what I'm saying.'

'No,' he said.

'But what's the alternative?'

He was silent, his features frozen; a face carved out of granite.

'But you're still young, Gary. You've got your whole life before you.'

His eyes had become cold and distant. She felt herself starting to panic.

'I'm sure they'll understand, once they know the reason you killed him.'

'No. Don't *you* understand? I'm a soldier.'

His words ground into her. Why? she asked herself. Why had she become his lover knowing deep down that it was just for one night?

*   *   *

Lambert swung open the front door, then stopped and looked back at Helen. 'Thanks for your help, sweetheart.'

'And?' she said.

'And for the lovemaking. As good as it always was. In other words, out of this world.'

'Flatterer.'

'Listen, I don't have time to talk now, but for Natasha's sake . . .'

She shook her head disbelievingly. 'That's moral blackmail.'

He gestured helplessly, hands palms up.

'And Natasha's a young adult,' she added.

'Please, Helen. Please. Don't let's chuck it all away.'

She found his wheedling tone annoying and she shook her head forcefully. 'No, Harry. It won't work.'

'Even murderers get a second chance now.'

'Yes but they can change. Whereas you –'

'I give you my word, sweetheart . . .'

She laughed humourlessly. 'Your word!'

'Just offer me a glimmer of hope and I promise I'll change. Just tell me I've got a chance.'

She held the balance of power now and she intended to make the most of it.

'OK,' she said. 'We'll see.'

Lambert gave her a grin before vanishing into the gloomy morning after.

*   *   *

Uninhibited in his nakedness, Evans climbed out of bed and walked over to the window.

'It's getting light,' he said.

She watched his body movement. He was like a prowling jungle cat, nerves tense and coiled, ready to spring into action. She shivered, wanting him back in the warm and comforting bed beside her.

'Gary, please, come back to bed. I want you to hold me again.'

Evans ignored her and drew back the curtains a fraction. Across the other side of the road, he saw a blue-uniformed figure slipping behind a tree. He squinted and focussed on the tree, staring at it for ages. Then he saw a rifle barrel sliding into place beside the tree trunk. He let the curtain fall back into place, grabbed his clothes and began to dress hurriedly.

Gwyneth sensed the impending danger, saw the bayonet glint in his eyes.

'Gary! What is it?'

'Don't worry,' he told her. 'You'll be all right.'

He finished dressing and started downstairs. She leapt out of bed, scrambled into her denims and a sweatshirt and followed him.

Chapter 19

It took Lambert ten minutes to get to police headquarters. He abandoned his car in the car park, leaving the keys in the ignition, in case any of the staff needed to move it, and ran over to join Ellis and Wallace, who were waiting by the high-powered Rover. Lambert threw open the rear door and was about to get in when he heard Ellis telling Wallace, 'Give me the keys, constable. I'll drive.'

Wallace looked like a child about to lose a bag of sweets and started to protest. 'Yes, but . . .'

'Quick!' snapped Ellis urgently, snapping his fingers at the young detective. 'We haven't got time to argue.'

Wallace still hesitated and looked towards Lambert for help. 'But Sergeant Ellis has got a problem with speed, sir.'

Lambert glanced at Ellis's tense, determined face. He had to make a split-second decision. He didn't have time to indulge Kevin's wounded feelings.

'OK,' he said. 'You drive, Tony.'

Lambert caught Wallace's sick expression before diving into the back seat. Ellis gunned the accelerator and they screeched out of the courtyard, the needle touching sixty in a moment.

'At least there's not much on the road yet,' said Ellis, swerving to avoid a postman on a bicycle.

He drove fast but skilfully, and Lambert wondered where he'd gained the experience. Maybe he hadn't. Perhaps this was a previously undiscovered prowess brought on by the adrenalin rush. Tyres screeched and burned as he raced the car over a roundabout just outside Swansea and then took it up to one hundred and twenty miles an hour on the M4.

Kevin shrank down into his seat and he pressed his foot

hard to the floor, stamping on an imaginary brake. Like many a fast driver, Kevin was a terrible passenger and hated being driven at speed. He could feel a lump in his throat like a boiled egg and he wondered if he could keep down the piece of toast he'd hurriedly eaten for breakfast.

'I hope this isn't a wild goose chase, sir,' he said, trying to disguise the tremor in his voice. He spoke mainly for his own benefit, to stop himself imagining the consequences of Ellis's driving. 'I mean, why would he want to go to this librarian's house?'

Lambert, his legs aching from the pressure of keeping them pressed to the floor to stop himself being hurtled about on the back seat like the waltzer at Barry Island, said, 'I've no idea, constable. But I think that's where he's gone. I tried ringing her and there was no reply. What does that suggest to you?'

'That the phone's been unplugged?' offered Wallace.

Lambert stared at his reflection in the driving mirror. His face was drawn and pale and there were purple bags under his eyes. He felt responsible for Gwyneth Chandler's safety. He should have acted on Helen's information sooner instead of being sidetracked into spending the night in bed with her. Was trying to repair a broken marriage an excuse for falling down on the job? Possibly. If there was a slim chance that she might take him back. But he had to own up to the fact that his first thoughts on seeing Helen last night had been purely carnal.

'Think he'll use her as a hostage, sir?' asked Ellis.

'I should think it's almost inevitable,' answered Wallace through gritted teeth as Ellis accelerated out of a bend.

Lambert snapped at him, 'Speculation DC Wallace. And didn't I ask you to do something for me before you came down with your . . . "virus"?'

He gave heavy emphasis to 'virus', suspecting that it was Kevin's excuse for a hangover.

'I managed to get the . . .' began Wallace, while Ellis slammed the gear into third as they hurtled towards a T-junction . . . 'info yesterday afternoon . . .' The engine whined protestingly as they screeched to a halt, then they turned sharp right and Ellis stamped on the accelerator. 'I felt a bit better by the afternoon, like.' He took a sheaf of papers out of his pocket and handed them over. 'Copies of his bank statement. Had to get a magistrate's warrant to get it.'

Lambert glanced at the statements. 'So, fifteen grand went out of Evans's account just before we pulled him in.'

Wallace chuckled. 'And that's not all. Have a look at the next sheet. That'll tell you who the recipient was.'

*　　　　*　　　　*

Evans put on his anorak, took the cap gun out of the pocket and weighed it in his hand. It seemed ridiculously light. But from a distance it would look real enough. Gwyneth came hurriedly down the stairs and took a pace back when she saw the gun.

'Gary, what . . . what are you doing?'

'Sit down at the table. I told you: you'll be OK.'

She was glad he'd ordered her to sit. There was no strength left in her legs and she could taste sickness on the base of her tongue. She sank into one of the chairs and swallowed rapidly. Tears of alarm began to blur her vision.

Evans went over to one of the windows and looked out of a chink in the curtain. A loudhailer burst through the still morning.

'Gary Evans. Can you hear me? Can you hear me, Gary? We know you're in there. We want you to give yourself up. We can settle this without anyone getting hurt. If you're armed, put your weapon down and come out with your hands on your head. We can sort this out without anyone getting hurt. D'you understand, Gary? We want to help you.'

Through her tears, Gwyneth watched Evans as he

164

considered this. 'Please, Gary,' she said. 'You can't fight them all. Not single-handed.'

He turned and grinned at her. The grin was more of a grimace, an expression of pain. 'That's what I'm here for,' he said.

*   *   *

'Hold tight,' shouted Ellis as the car sped towards a hump in the road.

Wallce dug his nails into his palms as the front wheels left the road. The car bounced back down onto the tarmac and he unclenched his fists. Lambert peered at a signpost as it flew past.

'Not far now. Five minutes top whack.'

'D'you think he's armed, sir?' asked Ellis.

'Well, if he is, we've got the Seventh Cavalry surrounding him.'

'Think there's any chance we could take him by surprise?'

'I doubt it. I think he's expecting us.'

Wallace turned his head towards Lambert with a questioning frown.

'You see,' Lambert explained, 'we've done everything he wanted us to do. Right from the word go.'

*   *   *

The croaking voice from the loudhailer repeated almost verbatim the same message. Evans stared at Gwyneth. He seemed to be deliberating. She wondered if there was a chance he still might be persuaded to give himself up. He opened his mouth to speak, but his voice seemed to catch in his throat. She waited.

'When we made love last night,' he said, 'is there any possibility you could have a baby?'

Dazed and confused, she shook her head. 'After I had my second daughter, I got myself sterilised.'

'Good. That's as it should be.'

The enormity of what he was about to do was like the stab of an ice pick in her spine. But before she could summon the strength to speak, he waved the gun in her direction and screamed,

'OK! Hit the floor! Now! Under the table! Do it! Get down!'

She scraped the chair back and fell to her knees, scrambling for safety beneath the table. As she clutched herself into a tight, self-protecting ball, the last thing she saw were his feet at the door.

Evans came running out of the cottage brandishing the cap gun just as the Rover hurtled and skidded to a stop at the bottom of the steep bank. When Lambert spotted Evans with the gun, something clicked in his memory and a young boy's voice said, 'I hope my cap gun's still there . . . It's gone . . . Some fucker's nicked my gun.'

Lambert threw open the car door and ran towards Evans. The police marksmen, he guessed, would be positioned behind the trees opposite the cottage. If he could get between them and Evans . . . It was a terrible risk, he realised. A gamble. There was a fifty-fifty chance it could be a real gun. But it all happened in a split second. No time to think. Instinct took over.

Evans spotted Lambert coming towards him and he knew the detective had guessed about the gun. He stopped running, got into firing position, slowly and deliberately raised the gun and aimed it at the detective.

What Lambert saw next was like something out of a dream. Evans's body jerked like a puppet and his body left the ground. It happened faster than a flash bulb popping but the image that stayed with Lambert seemed to slow the action. The loud report of the rifle came as the SAS man's body slammed into the bank. There was a large wet stain on his anorak, his arms thrashed about loosely, then his body bounced and rolled down the bank and into the road.

Lambert walked cautiously towards the body. He felt Ellis and Wallace close behind him, Ellis saying, 'You all right, sir?'

From behind a parked car further down the road, a uniformed police officer, brandishing a handgun aimed low at Evans's body, shouted angrily without looking at Lambert, 'What the fuck are you trying to prove? Fucking idiot. Nearly got yourself killed.'

Lambert climbed the bank and retrieved the cap gun. He showed it to the officer, who by now was joined by at least a dozen others. Lambert clicked the trigger.

'It's a child's cap gun,' he told them.

'And you knew about that?' the uniformed officer yelled accusingly. 'Why weren't we told?'

Lambert didn't reply. How could he admit it was supposition?

A medic stooped and checked Evans's pulse then pronounced him dead. Lambert turned and saw Gwyneth Chandler hobbling tearfully down the path that led to the road. A WPC ran to comfort her, keeping her away from the body.

'I'm all right,' Gwyneth sobbed.

She broke through the crowd which now circled Evans's corpse, looked down at the body and shuddered; then looked up at Lambert, accusation in her eyes, as if he was directly responsible for the killing.

'I'm sorry.' He showed her the cap gun. 'It was fake. We had no way of knowing. It's what he wanted. We were all part of his great scheme. His search for Valhalla.'

'Those who live by the sword,' she said. 'He told me.'

'What else did he say?'

The WPC put an arm around Gwyneth's shoulders.

'Look, I know it's been a terrible shock . . .' Lambert began.

The WPC threw Lambert an icy look and comforted Gwyneth, 'You don't have to . . .'

A great shuddering sigh shook Gwyneth's body, then she wiped the tears away from her cheeks and said, 'It's all right. I'll be all right. I'd sooner talk about it.'

'Thanks,' said Lambert quietly, and gave the WPC a reassuring nod. He took Gwyneth gently by the arm and they walked a little way down the road. She was frowning hard, staring at the ground, trying to make sense of it all.

'Why?' she asked simply.

'Lindow Man.'

She looked up at Lambert, eyes widening in surprise. 'How did you know about Lindow man?'

'Years ago my wife took me to the British Museum in London. I think Evans thought he was like Lindow Man, the Celtic warrior, the sacrificial victim. And I think he's staged his own elaborate suicide. The way a soldier dies.'

She forgot about her terrible shock for a moment and looked up at him, surprised and captivated by the revelation, like a religious fundamentalist gaining a convert.

'I owe you an apology, inspector.'

'Oh?'

'Yes, I'd sort of written you off as . . . well . . . a bit blinkered. I'm sorry, I didn't mean blinkered exactly . . .'

Lambert smiled at her. 'You don't have to apologise. I often give that impression. Maybe I should get out more often.' He inclined his head towards the cottage. 'So tell me about what happened in there?'

Gwyneth dropped her eyes, avoiding his look.

'That's if you feel up to talking about it.'

'I'm all right.'

'What did he tell you?'

'That farmer he shot. It was his father.'

'Yes, we know.'

168

She looked up sharply. 'You knew?'

'We only just found out – days ago. Checked the family's blood groups.'

'Poor Gary. Knowing he was the son of the man who raped his mother. It's no wonder he . . .'

'Did he say anything about the actual murder? Describe it in any way?'

Gwyneth frowned as she thought about this. 'It was weird but . . . he said he couldn't go through with it. And he seemed ashamed, as if the soldier in him had failed.'

'You'd swear to that?'

Gwyneth hesitated. 'Well . . . yes . . . although he seemed to change his mind after he told me. Said he *had* killed his father.'

Gwyneth watched Lambert carefully as he became embroiled in his own conflicting thoughts now.

'What's wrong?'

'About the time Wilson was shot, I was investigating a murder which was clearly a suicide and false confession.'

'I'm not with you.'

'It doesn't matter. It's just that it was staring me in the face, and I ignored it'

Gwyneth noticed how animated he became. He looked as if he was straining at the leash to get away. He glanced at his watch and gave her an apologetic smile.

'Mrs Chandler, I'm afraid I . . . If you don't mind, I'll get someone to look after you. And we'll need a statement, of course. When you feel up to it.'

'Before you go . . . you made me a promise.'

'Did I?'

'Yes. About his letters.'

'Oh yes. I'll make sure you get them back.'

She noticed he hadn't mentioned bringing them back himself, as he had the time before.

Chapter 20

There was a fine drizzle covering the Mumbles. A north wind blew down from the mountains and the rain had an icy bite to it. Lambert turned up his coat collar, and walked around the front of the car towards Terry Clark's house. Ellis let the window down and called out,

'Good luck, Harry.'

Lambert didn't turn back to acknowledge it. He walked, shoulders hunched, up the front path and rang the bell on Clark's front door. After a few minutes, just as he was about to ring again, the door was opened by the young mercenary. He was smartly dressed in a double-breasted, pin-stripe suit, a pale-blue shirt and a lemon-yellow silk tie. Lambert thrust his ID under Clark's nose. It was waved nonchalantly aside.

'No need for that, inspector. I don't suppose this is a formal visit. Like to come in?'

As Lambert went through into the living room, Terry Clark grinned confidently and said, 'I thought you might come back.'

Lambert halted. 'Oh? And why's that Mr Clark?'

'I thought you might be coming to give me the bad news. But I heard it on the local radio. Yeah, I shall miss old Gary. Poor bastard. But it was a forgone conclusion. Know what I mean?'

As Lambert sat on the arm of an easy chair, he noticed the passport and traveller's cheques on the coffee table.

'You going somewhere, Mr Clark?

'Nothing wrong with that, is there?'

'I could place you under arrest.'

Terry Clark looked genuinely puzzled. 'What the bloody hell for?'

'Murder. You shot Wilson.'

'Who the fuck is Wilson?'

'Gary Evans's true father.'

'You mean the bloke Gary shot was his old man?'

Clark looked shocked and surprised, but Lambert was unconvinced. He knew from his years in the police that Clark's reaction was just a fraction overdone.

'You know damn well it was his father.'

Clark crossed a finger on his breast and shook his head. 'On my mother's life.' He laughed and crossed behind the sofa. 'OK then, inspector, let's just say – for argument's sake – that I knew it was Gary's old man. It don't explain why I'd want to shoot him.'

'Because Evans couldn't go through with it. So he called you on his mobile and made you an irresistible proposition. Fifteen thousand pounds to kill his father. It was the easiest money you've ever earned for killing someone. You wiped your prints off the gun and left it for Evans to pick up. As you were leaving the farm, you almost collided with the car of the man who found the body. He identified your vehicle.'

Terry Clark came round to the coffee table, picked up the passport and cheques, and said, 'He must've been mistaken. I was here all night.'

'Neighbours would know if you went out. We can check.'

'So what? I might've popped out. Then again, I might not. For fuck's sake, it was more than two months ago. Who can remember?'

'What was the fifteen thousand for that Evans transferred to your account that same night?'

Clark stuffed the passport and traveller's cheques into his inside pocket and glanced at his watch.

'I didn't even know he'd bunged me that money till I checked my account much later. I expect it was the same as leaving it to me in his will, like. Seeing as he was the end of his line, so to speak. No one else to leave it to.' He tapped the glass of his watch. 'Listen, inspector, I don't wanna be rude, but I got places to go. So if you wanna arrest me, either put up or shut up.'

Lambert stood up and moved closer to Clark. 'Evans confessed before he died. To his pen pal librarian. Told her everything.'

'Yeah, well, poor bastard's dead now, so he ain't gonna repeat it, is he?'

Clark stood, legs apart, looking relaxed and sure of himself, a trace of a smile in his expression. 'Right, if you've got no further questions, inspector. I have to get to Heathrow Airport and it's a long drive.'

Lambert walked to the doorway and said, 'If anyone had a justifiable reason for homicide, it was Evans. But you – you sell your services to the highest bidder. Have a good flight, Mr Clark. And try not to kill many women or children.'

Clark flushed angrily. 'What the fuck would you know about it? I've never killed no one under the age of sixteen.'

Lambert couldn't believe he was hearing this.

'Oh. That makes it all right then.'

*　　　　　*　　　　　*

Lambert slid into the passenger seat next to Ellis. He unclipped the tiny microphone from behind his tie.

'Did you catch all that?' he asked Ellis.

'Sure. But you didn't expect it to go any other way, did you?'

'No, but I had to give it my best shot. Still, at least I might sleep better knowing that one day Clark will get his.'

'He who lives by the sword, eh, Harry?'

'Something like that.'

Ellis put the car into gear. 'We going back to headquarters?'

Lambert stared thoughtfully into the distance. When he

spoke, his voice was flat, expressionless. 'Drop me at my flat, will you? I've got a phone call to make. I'll get a cab in later on.'

As they pulled away from Terry Clark's house, Ellis said, 'Doesn't always work out like that though, does it?'

'That's a bit cryptic for me, Tony. What doesn't?'

'Bad guys getting their comeuppance. There's no guarantee Terry Clark won't die of natural causes at a ripe old age.'

A short, dry laugh erupted then died in Lambert's throat. 'If I thought that . . .'

His unfinished sentence hung in the air like damp fog. They drove in silence for a while. Both thinking about it. Both troubled by it. After a while Ellis gave an embarrassed cough.

'Harry,' he began tentatively. 'Do you believe in God?'

'Politics and religion. We ought to save it for the pub.'

'I just mean, you know, maybe the evil in this life will be punished in another.'

'A couple of years ago, Natasha asked me if I believed in God.'

'And what did you tell her?'

'I said it depends on which day I'm asked.'

Ellis laughed spontaneously. 'If it's a wet Wednesday I must be an atheist.'

They arrived outside Lambert's flat. As his boss was getting out of the car, Ellis said, 'Thanks for letting me drive, instead of Kevin.'

'As long as it's put a few ghosts to rest. Drive carefully, sergeant.'

Before pulling away, Ellis watched him walking towards his flat. A loping, defeated walk. A man returning to an empty flat. There was no one to impress and the walk said it all.

*   *   *

With barely a glance at the shambles of his flat, Lambert picked up the phone and dialled Helen's number. She picked it up after only two rings.

'Yes, who is it?' she asked breathlessly.

'It's me,' he announced.

'Harry, I'm sorry . . .' She spoke hurriedly. 'I heard about the shooting on the radio. It must have been terrible. But at least that woman was unharmed. I know you probably feel like unburdening yourself, but I don't . . .'

'That's not why I rang,' he cut in quickly. 'It's about last night . . .'

He heard a jangling sound, like a bunch of keys rattling.

'I've got a taxi waiting. I'm sorry – I don't have time to talk. I really don't.'

'I love you, Helen. I've never loved anyone else.'

'I'm going to miss my train.'

Her voice was firm. And cold.

'Didn't you hear what I said?'

'Yes, I heard you. But I don't have time to talk now. I'm going to Tom and Vanessa's in London for a couple of days. To look around.'

He froze. Somewhere in the back of his mind there echoed an empty, jeering laugh.

'I might go back to live in London,' she said. 'It's not definite. But I'd like to be near to Natasha if that's where she decides to settle.'

'And what about last night?' His voice became strident. 'What was all that about?'

'I don't have time to discuss it now. I'll miss my train.'

'This is more important than your bloody train,' he yelled. 'Catch the next one.'

'I'm going now. I'll talk to you when I get back.'

He felt himself spinning out of control and could do nothing about it.

'Shall I tell you what it was about, sweetheart?' His voice

hard and brittle, like the Hollywood tough guy. Knowing he would regret saying it, but he couldn't stop himself. 'Revenge. You're getting your own back, aren't you?'

The line went dead. He stared at the receiver for a moment as if he didn't quite believe what had happened. Then he hung up, and stared at his reflection in the cracked art deco mirror which hung on a chain over the hideous grey-tiled fireplace. The face which stared back at him needed reassurance, a defiant gesture of some sort.

'So that's final,' he told it. 'You always did have a way with women.'

Then, like an alcoholic reaching for a bottle, he looked up Gwyneth Chandler's number and started to dial.

THE END